The Final Siren

Nicki Edwards

DEDICATION

To Zac and Aimee Smith

Friends who became family, all because of a game called footy and

a team called the *Cats*.

To Eden and Baby Number Two.

And to Indy, an incredible and much-loved dog who recently

walked the rainbow bridge.

Acknowledgements

2020. The Year of The Nurse. The year of Covid-19. The year I turned 50 (without a party). The year when not much makes sense.

It's been a hard year to focus on writing, and there have been numerous times I've wanted to permanently close the lid of my laptop. If it wasn't for my readers who send me lovely encouraging notes, I might have given up.

But as my husband says, "it's not over until the fat lady sings." (An opera reference in case you're wondering.)

So, 2020 isn't over. Covid-19 isn't over. And my writing journey isn't over.

With the love of my local writer friends, Lisa Ireland, Delwyn Jenkins, Ellie O'Neill and Alli Sinclair; and with the unwavering support of Annie Seaton who has generously given her time and expertise yet again, I've managed to write more than I dreamed this year.

I also want to thank Belinda Williams who writes the best blurbs in the business, and Andrea Grigg who is the best writer friend a girl could dream of.

If you've read the acknowledgements in any of my previous books, you know my biggest supporters (and those I love the most in the world) are my family.

So, again, thank you Jeremy, Chloe, Zach (and Naomi) and Toby. It's been a big year of change for all of you and I'm so proud of how you've navigated huge interruptions to your plans. You are all incredibly resilient and positive and I love how you've embraced new seasons and directions during what will undoubtedly be the most difficult time of your lives. Soon, we will go back to "precedented" times (whatever they are) and I can't wait to see where you end up. I'm just looking forward to restrictions being over so we can gather together for a big group hug (without masks).

And finally, to Tim. My number one cheerleader in everything I do. I honestly do not know how you put up with me, but I'm glad you do. You clean up after me, you finish my sentences, you read my mind, you never roll your eyes - that I know of - and you love me unconditionally. Thank you for doing life with me, for continuing to dream of our future, for going along with my crazy hare brained ideas (like getting a horse), and for never putting pressure on me to be anyone other than "me" - as messy as that sometimes is. I adore you.

For a chance of happiness, will they follow their hearts?

Jed Delaney is a household name and considered one of the best ruckmen in the AFL. But after a devastating career-ending injury, he's faced with returning to the small town of Glengarrick to figure out what comes next.

Georgina Purcell always wanted to leave Glengarrick, but ten years after Jed left town taking a secret with him and breaking her heart in the process, she's still stuck wondering what her future holds.

When Jed walks back into Georgie's life acting like nothing has changed, sparks fly. But their feelings for one another can't change Jed's painful secret…that Georgie might be the reason for his retirement from the game he loves.

Will the lure of a new opportunity within the AFL be too much for Jed to walk away from? Or can he leave it all behind for a chance of happiness with Georgie?

Prologue

Ten Years Earlier

'Georgina? Darling, are you on your way home yet?' Mum's voice came through the speaker on Georgie Purcell's phone propped in the cupholder on the dash.

'Yeah, Mum, I'm on my way.'

'So's the storm.'

A deep low-pressure system was driving rain across the southeast of Victoria and damaging winds were forecast in the alpine region where Georgie lived in the town of Glengarrick. Gusts were expected to be around one hundred and twenty kilometres per hour, bringing blizzard conditions to the nearby mountains. Georgie was heading home that way, and the high risk of falling trees across the dark back roads scared her.

'Tell Zara to drive carefully.'

Georgie bit her bottom lip as she gripped the steering wheel tighter. She hated lying to her mum. 'Zara *always* drives carefully,' she said. At least *that* wasn't a lie.

Zara had been the first in their group to get her license and she loved running them around in her second-hand Toyota, a present from her parents on her eighteenth birthday. Georgie still had another eighty-four hours to go until she reached the State-required one hundred and fifty driving hours before she could get her license.

She also had another six months to wait until she turned eighteen and was legally old enough to be behind the wheel.

Georgie pushed those thoughts from her mind. She was familiar with this back road and although the rain was making it slippery and hard to see, nothing bad was going to happen.

She was in Zara's car, on her way home, like she'd told Mum, but Zara wasn't with her. Her best friend was staying the night with someone in Stockton, a neighbouring town. Zara didn't want her parents to know where she was, so she'd concocted a plan and roped Georgie in to go along with it.

The girls had driven together to Stockton and Georgie had dropped Zara to her new friend's place. She was now driving back to Glengarrick, alone. The plan was for her to leave Zara's car parked behind the pub and walk home. Tomorrow, Zara's friend would drive her back to Glengarrick.

Zara had told her parents she was staying the night at Georgie's and if they asked why her car was parked at the pub, she would tell them she'd had a drink and they'd walked back to Georgie's. As far as Zara was concerned, the plan was practically foolproof. Georgie went along with it, because when it came to Zara, that's what she always did.

As Zara had reminded her a dozen times, all Georgie had to do was get from Stockton to Glengarrick in one piece and without being stopped by the police. Thanks to the storm, the chance of running into the cops was basically zero. The one and only police officer in town would be over at the SES headquarters monitoring the weather.

'Where are you girls?' There was a note of worry in Jane's usually calm voice. 'It's really coming down in buckets here now and the wind is wild.'

Georgie flicked the wipers to their highest speed and squinted. Sheets of water slashed across her windshield and visibility was zero. Difficult enough for an experienced driver. Almost impossible for a learner. But she was being safe, not stupid, driving well below the speed limit. Tonight, the half hour trip was taking twice as long as it should because of the weather.

'Georgina?'

'I'll be home in half an hour or so, Mum, maybe longer.'

Georgie checked her speed. She was only going sixty in a hundred kilometre an hour zone. At this rate, she wouldn't get home for another forty-five minutes at least.

'Are you sure you're okay? I knew I shouldn't have let you girls drive tonight.'

Georgie's fib was that she and Zara were driving into Stockton to buy ink for the printer. It was a lame excuse, but the only one she could produce at short notice. Glengarrick had a newsagent that sold ink, but it wasn't open until Monday morning.

'I'm fine, Mum. Almost at the bridge.' The bridge was only five kilometres from town, but right now it felt further than the moon.

'Don't cross it if the river's up,' Jane warned.

'It won't be up,' Georgie said. 'There hasn't been that much rain.'

'Be careful.'

'Always.'

That wasn't a lie either. Among her group of friends, Georgie was known as the sensible one. The fact she was driving her best friend's car without a license was so far from "sensible Georgie", it almost made her laugh.

A gust of wind buffeted the little car and Georgie eased her foot off the accelerator and gripped the steering wheel tighter. She had plenty of time to get back to the pub, drop the car and run home. No need to hurry.

She'd only passed one other car on the road, the headlights blinding her momentarily, but that had been more than five minutes ago. It was pitch black, and she couldn't see anything when she looked out the window apart from the white lines on either side of the road illuminated by her headlights. She wasn't sure what was pounding harder and faster—the rain on the roof of the car, or her heart.

The creek was up ahead, and she slowed when the road dipped as it headed into the gully towards the bridge. Hopefully, there wouldn't be any water over the road.

Rain was coming down in torrents now, blurring her vision. The windshield wipers whipped back and forth over the window, but they weren't doing a thing. The road felt slick beneath her tyres as if it was covered in oil. Georgie clutched the wheel tighter, but when one of the front wheels hit a pothole and bounced, the car aquaplaned. She took her foot off the accelerator and held her breath. Her stomach plummeted, and her heartbeat thrummed in her ears. As her headlights picked up the metal guardrail she searched for the road, but it was gone, replaced by swirling water. Where was the bridge?

Two blinding lights suddenly appeared and with a jolt Georgie realised another car was heading towards her, coming across the bridge. The car hit the water and kept coming, almost bouncing across the road. Heart racing, breathing ragged, she yanked the steering wheel hard to the right so that the passenger side faced the oncoming car. Then she closed her eyes and prayed.

Images of her life flashed through her mind like a slideshow on fast forward—images of her parents waiting at home for her, her friends, her future.

The other car hit the side of hers with so much force it pushed her towards the fast-flowing creek. She screamed as her car went nose first down the gully into the water then flipped over, tail first. As the car flipped again, the windows and airbag exploded, and the coppery taste of blood filled her mouth.

The last thing Georgie saw was a tsunami of muddy water cascading over the car like a waterfall before everything went black.

Chapter 1

Current Day

In football, two types of hits existed: the kind players saw coming and the kind they didn't. Moments earlier, a human freight train had hit Jed Delaney side on, knocking him to the ground. The hit had snapped his head back and pain had roared up and down every nerve ending in an instant. When he landed, it felt heavy and unforgiving, like someone had crushed every bone in his body.

For a split second everything went silent—even the crowd—and in those breath-holding moments, Jed couldn't remember where he was or why he was there.

He slowly lumbered to his feet. The runner and doctor were jogging towards him in their high vis vests, concern written on their faces. Jed gave them a double thumbs up and tried to act unfazed. He removed his mouthguard and grinned. His teeth were still intact. He was fine.

Except he probably wasn't. That was one heck of a bump.

'I'm okay,' he said, shuffling towards them. 'I don't need to come off.'

Drew, the club doctor, shook his head. 'No choice in the matter, Delaney.'

He escorted Jed, grumbling, from the ground.

On the sidelines, Jed swigged water from the bottle offered to him, swirled it in his mouth and spat it out, all while keeping his gaze fixed on the game. The game he loved. His job. And the only thing he'd known for the past ten years.

Drew blocked Jed's view of the ground and clicked his fingers in front of Jed's face. 'Delaney.'

Jed smiled and put on his best "don't worry" expression. He'd had enough knocks and bumps over the years. Today's hit had been hard, but it hadn't been as bad as the one at the start of the season. *That* one had knocked him cold for ten minutes.

Jed had no recollection of what had happened. What he knew about it came from watching the replays and from what his coach and teammates had told him. Mum said she hadn't watched him play footy since.

'What year is it?' Drew asked.

'The year we're going to win another premiership.'

Drew gave him a lop-sided grin. 'Month?'

'July…the twenty-second,' Jed added, because that would be Drew's next question. 'And it's Saturday.'

He moved so he could see past Drew. They were down to the

final ten minutes and Geelong were only up by six points. At this rate, it was anyone's game and after last weeks' loss, they needed the win.

Drew whacked Jed's bicep with his clipboard. 'Oi. Focus. You're not going to miss anything. Answer my questions, then you can sit on the bench for a bit and catch your breath.'

Annoyed, Jed jogged on the spot to keep warm. 'I told you, mate, I'm okay. Bit rattled, but my head is fine.' He wanted to get out there and finish the game so he could enjoy a victory lap with the boys when it was over.

Drew's smile disappeared, and Jed stilled and withheld an exasperated sigh. Answering inane questions and proving he could stand on one leg like a flamingo without falling over was important to show the coach his brain hadn't turned into an omelette.

Management of concussion in the Australian Rules Football League had changed a lot over the past ten years Jed had been playing, and with good reason. Head impacts were associated with brain injuries and sometimes it wasn't clear whether a player had a mild concussion or a more serious head injury. Being taken off the ground was the first step. If Drew had any concerns, he'd refer Jed to another doctor for a more thorough assessment and he'd spend the rest of the game in the rooms; the last thing any player wanted.

'I'm going to ask you a few questions.'

Jed nodded. He knew the drill.

'What venue are we playing at today?'

Jed smirked. 'Docklands. Etihad. Marvel Stadium. They keep changing the name of the ground. How am I supposed to keep up?'

'Which quarter is it now?'

'Fourth. Final.'

'Who kicked the last goal?'

Jed grinned. 'I did.'

As a ruckman, Jed typically didn't kick a lot of goals, but he'd kicked two today. He described his job as a bit like a centre in basketball. He had to control the ball by tapping it out with his palm or fist during ball-ups or boundary throw ins. Ruckmen were tall—usually over two hundred centimetres—and Jed was one of the tallest in the AFL at two hundred and five.

And, according to the commentators, one of the best. Not that he'd ever let that go to his head, except on days like today, when he was playing well and showing them all that the knock to his head earlier in the season was nothing to worry about.

Drew grinned back. 'Yeah, you did.' He slapped Jed on the back. 'Good job.'

Rucking was one of the most physically demanding positions on the ground, both in terms of fitness and physicality. As a result of the high level of body contact when opponents clashed in the air, injuries were expected. In his ten years of playing at AFL level for Geelong, Jed had managed to remain mostly injury free, until the start of this season. Everyone wondered if his luck had run out, but he refused to entertain negative comments.

'Who did we play last week?' Drew asked.

'The Hawks.'

'Did we win?'

Remembering the humiliating loss, Jed screwed up his face. They'd been smashed, and no-one had anticipated it. 'No.'

Jed then repeated words back to Drew and recited a series of numbers—counting backwards from one hundred by nine. When he lifted one foot off the ground, his knee twitched, which set him off balance, but he recovered quickly. He was used to commanding his body to obey.

'Scale of one to ten. Pain? Headache?'

'Zero,' Jed lied. The pain brewing at the base of his skull, where the occipital nerve joined with his spine, was at least a six. But nothing a good massage after the game wouldn't fix.

'Any dizziness?'

Jed turned his head slowly left to right. 'All good. Maybe a two.' It was more like a five.

'Blurred vision?'

The fuzzy white spots swimming in front of his eyes were nothing to worry about, and if he didn't blink too much, they didn't multiply.

Drew's brows drew into a deep V. 'I think you should sit out the rest of the game.'

'Why?' Jed growled. 'Come *on.*' He glanced up at the scoreboard. Five minutes plus overtime.

'It won't kill you.'

Jed slumped onto the bench. Problem was, if he kept playing with a head injury, it might.

***

It was a close game, but one they should have won. Instead, they had their second loss of the season and it stung. But not as much as it would hurt on Monday when their coach ripped into them at training.

Cooling down in the locker room after the game, Jed couldn't shake the feeling something was wrong. It had nothing to do with the match—it was something else. Something he couldn't identify. Something he wasn't sure he could talk about with any of the guys stretching their hammies, or removing tape from ankles, knees and shoulders.

He sat on the hard bench, back pressed against the cold concrete wall, and took stock of his career. He loved footy, and at twenty-nine, he could easily keep going. Like Gazza, who was thirty-six and still going hard at it. But the head injury he'd sustained earlier in the season hadn't only shaken his brain, it had shaken his confidence. He hadn't mentioned it to anyone, but a question hovered continually in the background, like a shadow in his peripheral vision. And now, after another knock to his head, the unspoken question rose to the fore once again.

Should he retire?

Each week he was no closer to answering that question and after playing a great game and kicking two goals, retirement was the last thing he wanted to consider.

After showering, Jed shouldered his bag and headed for the car park. Outside, the usual rabble of reporters asked how the players felt about the loss. No-one was in the mood to talk, least of all Jed, but when he saw their captain smiling politely and responding to the media appropriately, he dragged in a breath. As a member of the leadership group, he needed to set a good example to the younger players.

Letting the other boys go ahead, he stopped and gave a brief answer to a question thrown his way.

'We'll get them next time.' It was the same line they gave after a loss when all they wanted was to get on the bus and go home.

'How are you feeling?' the reporter asked Jed. 'How's the head?'

'I'm great. No issues at all.' His phone rang.

Saved by the bell.

He held it up and gave the reporter an apologetic smile. 'Gotta take this, it'll be Mum.'

The reporter laughed and pushed her microphone in someone else's face.

In the bus on the way back to Geelong, Jed had no inclination to unpack the game with anyone. Slipping on his headphones, he closed his eyes and pretended to sleep.

***

Later that night, back in his waterfront apartment, where he lived alone, Jed made the mistake of flicking on the television. He usually avoided it at this time of year. They were at the pointy end of the season and every radio talk show, newspaper and footy show—and it seemed there was a footy show on every channel every minute of the day—wanted to comment on whether players would be dropped by their clubs at the end of the season. Until Jed's first knock at the start of this year there hadn't been any talk, not so much as a whisper, that his contract wouldn't be renewed. But tonight, his name came up. It was only once, and only briefly, and the journalist moved on quickly to talk about another player, but it was enough to make him sit up and listen.

The question had been what would happen if Jed Delaney got knocked out again?

He knew the answer because his coaches and the doctors had already warned him: he'd have to give up the game he loved. And if he did that, he had no idea what he'd do next. Life after footy was something he'd given little thought to.

Chapter 2

She was going to die. Closing her eyes, she dragged in a deep breath and held it, knowing what was coming. But miraculously, two hands reached down and grabbed her arms, yanking and pulling her from the car with such force it took what was left of her breath away.

Georgie woke, gasping for air as if she'd run a sprint. It was too early to be awake, but ten years' experience taught her there was no way she'd get back to sleep after a nightmare. Thankfully she didn't have them as often these days.

Her sheets were in a tangled mess and she kicked them back. Swinging her legs over the side of the bed she rested her elbows on her thighs and concentrating on slowing her breathing. After a minute, she got up and padded across to the bathroom to take a shower. Then she pulled on a pair of faded denim jeans, slipped on a white T-shirt, and pushed her socked feet into her leather Blundstones—her standard work uniform. Twisting her hair into a bird's nest on top of her head she was ready to go.

There wasn't much point bothering with makeup because there was no-one to impress in Glengarrick. She didn't worry about breakfast either, preferring to grab a coffee at the café as her standard first meal of the day.

Walking down the hall, Georgie paused at her mother's bedroom door and listened.

Nothing.

Slowly and quietly she turned the handle and peeked inside. The bedside table lamp was on, but her mother's eyes were closed and her breathing steady. Georgie wondered what time her mother had finally fallen asleep.

Shutting the door softly, Georgie retraced her steps to the kitchen. Grabbing her keys off the bench, she scribbled a quick note letting Mum know she was opening the café early. Not that she needed to. Her mother probably wouldn't notice she was gone unless Georgie didn't come home for dinner.

After all these years Mum still wore her loss like a veil. Georgie's parents, Rob and Jane, were a month shy of their thirtieth wedding anniversary when Rob was diagnosed with cancer. Diagnosis to death was so fast it had robbed the three of them the chance to do things as a family to create memories. Still dealing with her own grief, Georgie's spirit was further crushed as she watched her mum sink into a dark place and not be able to help her out of it.

As she drove to work, the navy-coloured sky turned a lighter shade of blue. Then streaks of orange, pink and yellow appeared on the horizon. It was a cold morning—the gauge on her car showed a snowflake symbol—and as the sun hit the grass, steam rose off the dew-covered paddocks. Georgie wasn't one to complain about the cold weather. She found these types of mornings invigorating.

She parked behind the café and stepped out of the car. Somewhere in the dark a dog barked twice. Unlocking the side door, Georgie let herself in. Dropping her bag in the tiny storeroom that doubled as her office, she walked through the café switching on the coffee machine, turning on the oven and heating, and flicking on the lights. The sun wouldn't appear on the horizon for another half an hour and not long after that the tables would be full. Most of her clientele were the same people she'd been serving since she was sixteen and had started working at the café for her parents.

Her parents had bought the Silver Spoon café when Georgie was in primary school, and over the years, she'd spent more hours here than she could count. Most nights after school, when she didn't have netball practice or when she wasn't hanging around the footy club watching the boy's training sessions, she had gone to the café, not home. She did her homework out the back while her parents prepped food for the next day. They'd been such happy times.

When she was old enough, she'd started working there part

time and it didn't take long to become everyone's bestie by making jumbo-sized thick shakes, or ice cream spiders, and sneaking free donuts or Mum's Yo-Yo biscuits to her school friends.

When she finished high school, Georgie was desperate to get out of town like everyone else. She moved to Melbourne to study nursing at university and she'd almost finished her degree and was applying for Graduate Year programs when her dad got diagnosed. She went straight home.

Now, nearly seven years later, she was still in Glengarrick, still working at the café and dreams of becoming a nurse were gone. Funny thing was, she no longer resented the small town life as much as she used to. It wasn't necessarily that she'd settled for second best, it was that she was no longer sure nursing was what she wanted to do. Running the café wasn't her life goal either, but for now, it was what she had. Until she knew what the next was supposed to be, she'd keep doing this with a smile.

Turning on the sound system, Georgie cranked up the volume, and sang along while she pulled cakes and slices from the fridge and put them in the glass-fronted refrigerated display cabinet.

Today was the start of her favourite weekend of the entire year: the Glengarrick Peak to Pub fun run was tomorrow morning, followed by the fireworks at night down by the river, and the footy Grand Final on Sunday. Everything stopped for this weekend and everyone in town got involved. Even people who hadn't lived here for years came back. They started arriving on Friday afternoon and didn't leave until the pub closed its doors late on Sunday night.

Georgie was out the back in the kitchen making sandwiches for toasties when the front door opened. Frowning, she glanced up at the clock. 6:25. Everyone knew she didn't open until seven.

Boots clicked across the wooden floorboards.

'Yoo-hoo. You here, Georgie Porgie?'

'Zazu!' Georgie dropped the bread she was buttering, flying out the front to meet her best friend.

They squealed and hugged each other tightly.

'Oh, my lordy, it's so good to see you,' Georgie said, giving Zara another tight squeeze. The last time her best friend had been home was Christmas and Georgie missed her like crazy. Zara Pritchard was more than a best friend. She was the sister Georgie wished she'd always had. They'd met on the first day of primary school when they were seated beside each other because their surnames put them side by side on the roll. They became firm friends from that moment and the rest was history.

Georgie released her grip on Zara's arms. 'You're up and about early.'

'Got home late last night. I was heading out for some fresh air when I saw the lights on. What are you doing here before the sun's up?'

'Couldn't sleep.' She didn't tell Zara she'd had another nightmare.

'You ready for the influx?'

'Hope so.'

Georgie glanced over her shoulder at the packed display cabinets. Reece, her chef, had been cooking up a storm during the last week and they were ready. Today they'd be swamped with people stopping in for breakfasts and brunches. Tomorrow after the fun run, crowds of runners and spectators would pack the café before heading down to the river with overflowing picnic baskets.

Zara followed Georgie out the back, grabbed a banana and hoisted herself onto a bench. She chatted a mile a minute while Georgie went back to making sandwiches.

'You ready for the run?' Zara asked.

'Absolutely. I have to beat my time from last year.'

Zara rolled her eyes. 'I don't know when you became so competitive. You weren't like this at school.'

Georgie laughed. 'A lot's changed since then.'

'Are you going to join us for the fireworks?' Zara asked.

'Wouldn't miss it for anything. It's my favourite day of the year.'

By the time the sun set on Saturday night, the banks of the river would be packed with locals laying on blankets waiting for the fireworks to light the night sky.

'And you'll come to the pub afterwards too?'

'I'll see.'

Usually families with kids went home once the fireworks were over and everyone else went to the Old Bush Inn, the only pub in town, which was owned and operated by Zara's parents.

'How cool that both the men's and women's teams have made it through to the Grand Final,' Zara said.

'It's awesome,' Georgie agreed, 'but it's a shame the girls are playing in Wangaratta on Saturday. It would have been so good if they'd played on Sunday at home before the boys. Then we could have watched both games.'

Georgie never missed a game, no matter how tired or hung over she was after a big night the previous night.

It was a milestone year for the local footy club with both the Glengarrick men's and women's teams making it through to the Grand Final. They were expecting a crowd of at least two thousand—double the size of the town—to watch the game on Sunday.

'This place looks great, George,' Zara said, gazing around. 'I love the new decor. Like something you'd find in Melbourne.'

Georgie looked at the café through Zara's eyes and her chest puffed with pride. She'd initially taken over running the café alongside her mum after her dad died but when Mum's health deteriorated, she'd had to step in and run it on her own. Last month she'd finally spruced up the space, painting walls and stripping and staining the timber floors. Zara's compliment was the boost she needed.

'How are your folks?' Georgie asked.

'They're great. Did you hear they're going to be grandparents in March?'

Georgie looked up. 'No. They kept that quiet. Who's expecting? Lou or Harry?'

'Both.' Louise and Harriet were Zara's younger sisters.

'How do you feel about that?'

'I'm fine, but I did hear Mum muttering something to someone that she's worried I'll end up a spinster.'

Georgie chuckled. 'Have you told them about Kath?'

Zara tossed the banana skin into the rubbish bin with the same ease she used to score goals in netball. 'Nope. And they're not about to find out yet.'

'You have to bring her home to meet the family one day.'

Zara and Kath had been an item for eighteen months and even Georgie hadn't met her.

Zara rolled her eyes. 'Can you picture the look on Dad's face?'

'Fair point.'

'Mum'll probably be okay with it, but Dad's old school.' Zara slid off the bench, grabbed a glass and poured herself a drink of water from the tap. 'I'll bring her back once we're married.'

Georgie stared at her friend. 'Is it that serious?'

Zara nodded. 'Yeah. I think so.'

'Wow. That's awesome. I'm happy for you.' She was happy, even though she felt a tiny stab of envy.

Zara elbowed her in the ribs. 'Your turn will come again.'

Georgie rolled her eyes. 'Trust me, I'm in no hurry to walk that road again.' *Thanks to Neil.*

Zara's face dropped. 'Does that mean you've given up internet dating?'

'Nothing to give up. I never got around to uploading my profile.'

'Georgiee,' Zara drawled. 'Last time we talked you promised me you'd do it.'

'In case you haven't realised, I've been a bit busy running a café.'

The door opened again, and Georgie looked up at the clock. Ten minutes until opening.

'I'll get it,' Zara said before Georgie could comment.

Georgie left her to it. Zara was more than capable of making coffees until Abbey, her barista arrived.

She looked up a few moments later when Zara entered the kitchen, grinning like a fat farm cat in a dairy.

'What?'

'I have a surprise for you.'

Georgie frowned. Zara knew she didn't like surprises.

Her friend's smile morphed into a grin as she held out her hand. Georgie took it reluctantly and followed her out of the kitchen. Entering the café, she froze. The entire gang from high school were there. Jack, Charlie, Kate, Ben, and Emma. Georgie shrieked and rushed over to hug everyone. She hadn't seen any of them since last year's Grand Final weekend. The only person missing was Jed, but he'd barely been back since the day after they'd tossed their graduation caps in the air.

Her friends hugged her in turn.

'How are you doing?' Charlie asked. 'And your mum? How's she going?'

Everyone knew about Georgie's mum.

'What's new in good ol' Glengarrick?' Emma asked.

They threw more questions at her and Georgie laughed. It was so good to have them here.

'I'm good. Mum's fine, and as for what's happening in Glengarrick? Other than this weekend, nothing.' She grabbed menus and handed them to Charlie. 'Breakfast is on me.' She started pushing tables together to form one large table in the corner.

Abbey arrived and went straight to the coffee machine while Zara ducked into the kitchen and offered to help Reece cook bacon and eggs with all the trimmings for everyone.

The next twenty minutes were busy—as they always were first thing in the morning—and Georgie didn't have a chance to check on her friends. But judging by the chatter and laughter coming from their table, they were all enjoying catching up. She'd have plenty of time over the weekend to see them and hear their news.

When the door opened again, she didn't look up. Instead she reached through the servery window to grab plates from the kitchen to take over to a couple near the window.

'Morning,' she called out cheerfully. 'I'll be right with you.'

The song playing through the speakers ended and a hush fell over the café as if everyone had stopped talking at once.

'Oh. My. God,' Abbey uttered in an almost reverent whisper. 'Do you know who that is?'

Georgie turned and the plates in her hands suddenly felt as heavy as kettle bells. Her mouth dropped open.

'Well, well, well,' Zara said, coming to stand beside Georgie. She put her hands on her hips and grinned. 'If it isn't Glengarrick's hometown hero.'

'Hey, Zazu. Hi, Georgie.'

Georgie forced her eyes up from the broad expanse of his chest to his face. She swallowed. 'Hey, Jed.'

He grinned. 'Good to see you.'

Chapter 3

A wave of heat washed over Georgie as if someone had opened the front door on a hot day. Jed Delaney was back in town, looking divine, and he was beaming at her as though he was pleased to see her too. A shiver raced up and down her spine. Jed looked no different.

It had been ten years since he'd left town and naturally Georgie had watched him on TV, but after everything he'd been through during the past year, she figured he might have aged, at least a little bit. But no, he was as undeniably boy-next-door drop-dead-gorgeous as ever.

And every bit as tall.

Georgie looked up—and up—and dark brown eyes framed by long dark lashes met hers from beneath his Geelong Cats peaked cap. His light brown hair stuck out from under the cap, curling on his collar. Even with the baggy jumper he wore, it was impossible to hide his size and musculature. Not just tall, Jed's chest was broad and his shoulders wide.

He offered her a tentative smile, revealing perfect white teeth. But as quick as he flashed them, they disappeared. Was he nervous or was she projecting her own feelings onto him?

Georgie licked her suddenly dry lips. 'Hey.' She tried to smile, but her cheeks felt tight and butterflies churned in her stomach as a deluge of memories swamped her. It was so good to see him after all this time.

At school, Jed was the kind of guy who flew under the radar. He hadn't liked drawing attention to himself which had been impossible given how tall he was. On the field though, he became a different person. Confident, bold and decisive. With his height, he could have played basketball, but he'd chosen footy and excelled at it, becoming the poster boy for the AFL for the past ten years. Georgie knew his resume by heart. He'd played in the ruck for the Cats and helped them win two premierships. He'd won the Norm Smith medal in one of those games, making him the best on ground in a Grand Final. And he'd been awarded a Carji Greeves Best and Fairest medal three years running at his club.

Everyone loved Jed Delaney, including those who'd never met him.

When they were at school, Jed never had trouble catching the eyes of the girls, but no-one had caught *his* eye. Except Georgie. A fact known only to the two of them.

Her body tingled as the repressed memories tried to surface.

She'd developed a king-size crush on Jed Delaney in year nine that hadn't faded despite everything that had happened. Judging by her racing heart, clearly ten years hadn't dulled those feelings one bit.

Georgie believed in soulmates. Zara used to tell her she was naïve, and her mother said she was a hopeless romantic, but Georgie had always believed in happy-ever-after endings. She'd believed in true love. Believed that everyone had a "someone" out there. And for years, she'd clung to a slim hidden hope Jed Delaney was her someone.

The last thing she needed was to have to deal with her infatuation while he stood in front of her. She could only hope that he couldn't see she still had feelings for him. If he could, he'd probably assume she'd succumbed to his brown-eyed charm like legions of other footy fans. Her cheeks scorched with embarrassment. Even if she was still interested in him, she was way out of Jed Delaney's league. He wasn't a world away from her everyday existence in Glengarrick. He was in a different galaxy.

Anyway, for all she knew, Jed could have developed a big ego and be nothing like the person she remembered. Sure, he still made her feel warm and tingly inside, but he might have changed. If he had, her infatuation would die a natural—and quick—death.

'Man, it's good to see you, Jed,' Zara said, coming to Georgie's rescue.

Zara gave him a hug, which he awkwardly returned. Like Georgie, Zara wasn't tall, and Jed had to fold himself in half to wrap his arms around her.

He released her as two girls entered the café. The moment they spotted Jed they stopped talking mid-conversation and stared at him, eyes wide. One of them, who couldn't be much older than sixteen, batted her fake eyelashes at him.

'Ladies.' Jed tipped his cap and flashed them a heart-stopping smile.

At least it felt like Georgie's heart had stopped for a second. She had no idea if Jed had that effect on everyone else, but the way the girls giggled, she figured they were as enamoured with him as she was.

Giggling, they stepped up to the counter.

'What can I get for you?' Georgie asked.

They took their time selecting take away muffins and ordering their coffees, snickering and glancing at Jed. Georgie's stomach knotted into a tight ball. She ignored them, but it was impossible to ignore Jed. She felt the burn of his eyes on her as she busied herself filling their orders and taking their payment.

When they left, they flashed flirtatious smiles at Jed, and he smiled politely back.

'You'll be all they talk about for the rest of the day,' Georgie said.

'Doubt it.' He leaned closer to Georgie and dropped his voice. 'I've only come to pick up a coffee for me and Mum. Any chance you can help me out, so I don't get trapped here of the next hour?'

Georgie glanced around. A few people had pulled out their phones and looked like they were about to tackle him for a selfie.

She smiled. There was no way he could fly under the radar now. Once word got out he was back, there was nowhere to hide.

'Your mum's order's ready,' she lied, coming up with the only thing she could think of to rescue him. She raised her voice so everyone could hear her. 'It's out the back. If you want to come with me, I'll grab it for you.'

His eyebrows knit together in confusion for a second, then relief crossed his face. 'Oh, yeah. Awesome. Thanks.' He turned around and tipped his cap. 'Good to see everyone.'

He followed her behind the counter and Georgie led him through the kitchen, motioning to Reece and Abbey to close their mouths, before taking him into her tiny office that doubled as the storeroom.

'It's good to see you, Jed,' she said with a smile after closing the door.

When he smiled back and took a step closer, her legs turned to jelly, and another wave of warmth washed over her making her feel like she'd stood up too quickly. If he got any closer, she'd be wearing his aftershave.

Don't look him in the eyes, she warned herself. *If you do, you'll drown in pools of melted chocolate.* Then again, if she had to die, that wouldn't be the worst way to go.

They stared at each other, neither of them saying a word. Time wound back, and they reached for each other at the same time. Before she had a chance to think through what she was doing, Georgie hugged him tight, inhaling the same intoxicating scent she remembered from the jumper he'd wrapped around her the night of the storm when he'd rescued her.

To her surprise, and delight, Jed hugged her back. But after a moment he cleared his throat. Georgie pulled back too, tucked her hair behind her ears and pretended some papers on the desk needed straightening.

'How's your mum?' she asked when he didn't say anything.

'Not going to ask how I am?'

She looked up and met his gaze. This time his smile lit his entire face and reached his eyes. That was better—the Jed she remembered.

'How are *you*?' she asked.

Jed squinted and stared over her shoulder before replying. 'Mum's good. So am I. Thanks for asking.'

She tilted her head. 'Are you *really* okay?' She'd always been able to read him and the evasive look over her shoulder was a dead indicator there was something bothering him.

His smile fell and when he looked back at her, there was something missing in his eyes. She instantly regretted asking the question. Everyone who followed Australian Rules Football knew he wasn't okay.

'I'm fine. Happy to be home, for now...' His voice trailed off.

She wanted to ask what "for now" meant but held back and he didn't offer any further information. The faraway look on his face was gone, replaced by his usual smile.

'You hungry?' she asked.

'That's why I'm here.'

Of course, that's why he was here; it wasn't like he'd come into the café looking for her.

Nodding like a fool, she backed out of the office. 'Let me get grab you a menu and you can pick what you want and stay here while I get it for you. That way you don't have to have everyone coming up and asking you for a selfie. Coffee too?'

'Please. Double shot, extra hot, latte.'

'Georgie?'

She stopped with her hand on the door handle. 'Yeah?'

He glanced down before lifting his head and looking at her again. 'Sorry to hear about your dad. I should have called.'

Her mouth went dry. It had been seven years since her dad died and not a word from Jed. Yeah, it would have been nice if he'd called, but it wasn't like they'd stayed in touch. She smiled. No hard feelings. 'You've been a little busy since you left town. But thank you.'

'It must have been tough for you.'

'It was.'

Still is.

Before he could say anything else, she dashed out, grabbed a menu, and handed it to him when she came back

'No rush. Take your time. I'll get Abbey to make your coffee.'

Back in the café, she dragged in a deep breath. Glancing at her table of friends, she was relieved to see none of them were paying her any attention. Their meals had been served and they were tucking into breakfast and laughing and telling stories and jokes the way they always did when they got together. She exhaled slowly and tried to steady her racing heart. She hadn't expected seeing Jed again would affect her this much.

'Georgie!'

She tuned back in as Abbey held out the takeaway coffee for Jed.

'You okay?' Abbey asked. 'You look like you've seen a ghost or something.'

She laughed off Abbey's comment. 'I'm fine. It's just weird having Jed in here after all these years, that's all.'

'Were you two friends?' Abbey asked.

'Yeah.'

They had been more than friends once, but no-one knew that.

'I've never heard you talk about him.' Abbey frowned. 'Everyone in town seems to have a Jed Delaney story except you.'

Georgie shrugged. Lots of people liked to think they knew Jed. Over the years when the media had come to town looking for stories, a few people hadn't thought twice about making things up in order to have their name in the paper. When anyone asked her,

Georgie simply replied that she and Jed went to the same school and left it at that. No-one needed to know anything else.

Georgie remembered the night the whole town—or at least that's what it felt like—went down to the pub to watch the draft on Foxtel. When Jed was announced as Geelong's number one pick, the crowd had exploded. The beer had flowed freely late into the night and she'd stood in the back of the room, full of an unexpected pang of sadness. Deep down she knew once he was gone, Jed wouldn't be coming back to Glengarrick.

She returned with his coffee.

He accepted it with a smile. 'Thanks, George. Menu looks good.'

Her cheeks warmed at the compliment. She and Reece had worked hard on the menu. 'I recommend the breaky burrito if you're hungry. Or the porridge with stewed apple and cinnamon with berries is delicious. Or if you're after something sweet, the peach Danishes are incredible, and we make our own croissants. Oh, and we have a selection of cakes and quiches in the display cabinet. Depends whether you're after something sweet or savoury. Or I could get Reece to make you a simple bacon and eggs take away.'

Why couldn't she stop gibbering?

'The breakfast burrito and a Danish sound great.' He handed the menu back to her. 'Is it okay if I hang here while I wait? It's not that I want special treatment, but to be honest, I didn't expect it to be so busy this early. I thought I could slip in and out without anyone seeing me.'

'Yeah, no worries.' She twisted the menu in her hands. Her tiny office suddenly felt smaller. 'I'll—ah—I'll put your order in with Reece.'

She backed out and went to the front. As she entered Jed's order into the computer system, she sensed Zara's eyes on her. She glanced over to the corner where her friends still sat.

'You okay?' Zara mouthed.

Zara was the only other person in the world who knew what happened that night. Well, not *everything*.

Georgie nodded, but she wasn't okay. She was far from okay.

And, if she had to guess, neither was Jed.

Jed's obvious discomfort had nothing to do with her. After ten years of playing for the Cats, the unthinkable had happened. Less than two minutes after the ball was bounced for the first game of this year's season, Jed was nudged in the back when he went up for a contest. He'd stumbled forward, colliding in a sickening crunch with another player and dropped to the ground like a felled tree.

Georgie had been at work, watching the game on television, and she'd dropped the meal she was carrying. The entire café had fallen silent, along with, it seemed, the entire MCG. Everyone held their breath, waiting for him to get up, shake himself off and keep playing, the way he usually did.

But Jed didn't move.

It seemed like an eternity before the buggy carrying the stretcher made it to him in the middle of the field and carried him away down the race to hospital. The last image was Jed giving a shaky thumbs up sign to the cameras.

He was only knocked out for a minute, but he reportedly lost all memory of the incident and the succeeding week. Three weeks later, after being cleared of concussion, he was back, but he only played half a game. The commentators revealed he'd admitted the knock had affected his memory and mobility and he hadn't been able to train to the level he'd wanted to. After that game he played every other one, but anyone could tell he wasn't playing his best.

It was all everyone in Glengarrick could talk about. Journalists showed up in town hoping to glean some information from Jed's mum, but she'd driven down to Geelong to be with him. Georgie wanted to reach out to him but had no way of contacting him. So, like everyone else, she waited. And waited.

Finally, two weeks later, after what seemed to be another innocuous knock to his head, an emotional Jed, flanked by his mother, Michelle, and his coach, revealed his heartbreaking decision at a press conference. At twenty-nine, he was retiring from the game he loved.

Once his order was ready, Georgie put it in a takeaway box and added two Danishes and a croissant to the bag. He looked like he could use some sweetening up and if he didn't want them, he could give them to his mother.

'You can go out the back door if you like.' She looked up at him. 'Or I can walk with you out the front. Not that I'm big enough to be your bodyguard but they're less likely to stop you for your autograph or a photo if you're with me.'

He chuckled. 'I'm all good, Georgie Porgie. I can look after myself.'

The use of her nickname made her smile. She followed him back through the kitchen into the café. He held up his paper bag of food. 'Thanks again for this.'

He was almost out the door by the time Charlie got to him.

'Hey, man,' Charlie said easily as he held out his hand. 'Good to see you again.'

Jed shifted the brown paper bag into his left hand and shook Charlie's hand. 'You too. How've you been?'

'Yeah. Good. Hey—listen—a bunch of us are hanging out tomorrow night to watch the fireworks after the run. You're welcome to join us.' Charlie looked across at Georgie. 'You're coming, aren't you?'

'Absolutely. Wouldn't miss it.'

Jed hesitated. 'I'll see what Mum's doing.' He glanced at Georgie then back at Charlie, then over to the group seated at the table watching him. 'It was great seeing you all. Guess I'll see you later.'

Charlie shook his hand again before heading back to the group.

Jed turned to leave, and Georgie grabbed his arm. Dropping her voice, she whispered, 'I really hope you can make it tomorrow night.'

'I'd like that. We have a lot to catch up on.'

As the words rolled off his tongue, a flush burned through her.

Don't be crazy, she warned herself. *You cannot think about Jed like this.*

But it was too late. He'd been here for less than ten minutes and already he was under her skin. Still.

Chapter 4

Jed crossed the street and returned to his car. While he ate the breakfast burrito—which tasted great—he took in the view of the bustling main street. Glengarrick was one of many small towns nestled between the mighty Murray River and the south-east coast of Victoria. It was a picturesque alpine town that appeared to have been forgotten by time. But in the ten years he'd been away, that had changed. It had doubled in population as Melburnians escaped the city for tree changes. House prices had escalated, and new shops and businesses had opened.

Yesterday as he drove into town, he'd been staggered by how many houses were being built in a subdivision that used to be a paddock. Both the primary school and high school had new buildings and a lot of the shops in the main street had been given a facelift.

Jed exhaled and lifted his eyes to the mountains in the distance. He remembered someone saying once that this view had the power to right wrongs, rewind time, and glue all the broken pieces back together. It was true. He told anyone who would listen that if they wanted to sort their head out, they should head to Victoria's High Country, a place of understated beauty, diverse landscapes, and some of the most genuine people on earth. For him, this little pocket of Victoria was the place where life had always felt simpler. Which was why he was thinking of coming back. Right now, he needed simple.

Concussion had changed him. It wasn't only a knock to the head. In its most severe form, it was an acquired brain injury that carried with it a host of side effects. Jed had experienced headaches, sleep deprivation, and dizzy spells. The doctors had also warned him he was at risk of depression.

At first, losing everything that came with playing footy had caused a deep loneliness to seep into the marrow of his bones, but gradually things were getting better. At first, stepping away from football and everything that came with it was like turning his back on the only world he'd ever known. He had nothing to work toward, nowhere to direct his discipline, no one relying on him. His teammates, who were basically his family, quickly moved on without him. That was the nature of the game.

He'd been lost for a while, and only those closest to him understood how tough it had been. He hadn't just lost his footy identity; he'd lost part of his identity as a person too.

He shoved the melancholy thoughts aside. He'd worked hard

to come to terms with his injury, to learn how to look forward, not back. He was glad to return home, despite what people probably thought. He'd had an incredible ten years in Geelong, and a phenomenal career, and he needed to remember and celebrate that.

Now was the time to work out what to do next: maybe what he should do was put down roots where he belonged.

As the son of a third-generation farmer, it had always been his understanding *Riverview* would be passed down to him. But that was before his father had gambled away their life savings, walked out on him and Mum, and landed himself in jail for fraud. Before football, Jed had imagined taking over the farm, falling in love, having a couple of kids, and settling down. But between dealing with his father debts, his parent's divorce, the threat of losing the farm, then his own issues caused by the concussion, things weren't going to plan.

He started the car and headed for the farm. Unfortunately, unless he could convince Mum to change her mind and let him help her out, there might not be a farm to take over. He hadn't given any consideration to what he'd do if there wasn't a farm to run after footy was finished. From the day he'd been recruited, he'd always known it wasn't a game he could play forever. He hadn't expected his career to end so soon. Or the timing of it to be out of his control.

As the reality sunk in, it had left him with lots of thinking time. Coming back home, he'd been surprised by some unexpected regrets. One of them was not staying in touch with his friends from school. Seeing them gathered around the table in the café and knowing he was no longer part of the group was hard.

Seeing Georgie again was harder. She used to be so calm and not easily rattled, but today she reminded him of a racehorse on a windy day. Either that, or she was yet another person who thought because he played AFL he was some kind of hero, and she'd been starstruck.

There was a third reason.

After that night of the storm, he'd barely spoken to her, so it was hardly surprising she'd acted weird.

Mum had told him that Georgie left town after school like the rest of them, but he'd never asked what she'd done after university, so he didn't know why she was back in Glengarrick.

When he walked in and saw her behind the counter, he'd been surprised. Not only to learn she'd taken over running The Silver Spoon from her parents, but by how incredible she looked. She'd always been a head-turner in the classic girl-next-door way, but she'd matured and grown from a pretty girl into a stunningly beautiful woman.

While they'd chatted, it had been hard not to stare at her. Her breasts had pushed teasingly against her slim fitting white T-shirt and her skinny leg denim jeans had hugged her womanly curves. After the phony women he'd met over the past ten years, it was nice to know there was still nothing fake about Georgie Purcell.

She still wore minimal makeup and her chocolate hair had the same natural caramel highlights she'd had in high school. She even wore it in the same high ponytail.

The knot in his stomach tightened and he rubbed at the ball of tension in the back of his neck. He hadn't expected seeing Georgie again would cause such a visceral response. And he hadn't anticipated coming home would release so many long-held memories. Memories that rushed up to greet him now.

What would have happened if he hadn't found her that night in the storm? He'd always had a secret crush on her, but he didn't know whether he would have acted on it if they hadn't been put in the position they had.

He shook his head to clear it. Thinking about Georgie and that night should be the last thing on his mind. Especially if he didn't know if he was planning on staying in town. He couldn't afford to get involved with her then leave again.

He exhaled loudly. Mum was right. At the rate he was going, he'd still be single by the time he hit thirty. Back in Geelong, playing footy, he could have had his choice of women, but he'd never indulged. Not that he'd been celibate, but he'd been cautious about who he dated. In his opinion, there was too much pressure on players to find a *WAG*. Not that all the wives and girlfriends of footy players chased after the near celebrity status of dating an AFL player, but plenty did, and he'd avoided them.

But if he moved back to Glengarrick permanently, the

likelihood of finding a wife was slimmer than his chance of playing footy again. If he had to guess, the only available women in town were either too young, too old, or already married. He sighed. Maybe he should try one of those online dating sites.

He pushed the thoughts aside and headed home. There was no point dwelling on the past or worrying about the future. He was here in town for one reason—to toss the coin at Sunday's Grand Final between the Saints and the Rovers—then he could decide whether he hung around or left again.

And that would depend on Mum.

***

Later that day, Jed swung himself up onto the seat of the tractor and wrapped his hands around the well-worn steering wheel. Even after all these years, it felt as familiar as a leather Sherrin in his hands. Working on muscle memory, he'd checked the spark plugs, inspected the fuel lines, ensured there was fuel in the tank, changed the oil and pre-lubricated the engine.

It was until walking into the shed and inhaling the musty scent of old hay that he realised how much he missed working on the farm. When Mum had told him some of the neighbour's cows had gotten through the wire and found their way in the orchard, he'd offered to fix the fences and had been surprised when she'd willingly accepted his help.

Pressing the brake, he depressed the clutch and willed the cantankerous old tractor to start.

Jed turned the key, and the tractor stammered and snorted but refused to start.

'Come on,' he growled, flipping the key back to the off position.

The tractor was yet another thing on the farm that needed replacing. It frustrated him no end that Mum wouldn't let him use his earnings to help her out. For ten years he'd been paid well for playing footy and he had more than enough money to do whatever it took to get the farm back on its feet. But Mum wouldn't hear of it.

He turned the key again and this time the tractor spluttered and popped, then roared to life, before rumbling with a steady purr. He patted the steering wheel as if it were a horse.

'Good girl. Looks like you'll live. For today at least.'

As he drove down the drive, the tractor lurched over the ruts and when he was bounced out of the seat a third time, he forced himself to slow down. The last thing he needed was an accident. He also mentally added re-gravelling and grading the driveway to the long list of things that needed doing around the farm.

Since the divorce, Mum had been forced to sell off acres of *Riverview* to pay for his father's gambling debts. Luckily, the old brick farmhouse was in her name because it had belonged to her parents, so she'd been able to keep that. She'd also managed to hold onto approximately a hundred and forty acres of undulating farmland that backed onto the river. There was so much potential and if only he could get Mum to see he didn't want to take the farm away from her, he wanted to help her run it.

It was hard seeing his mother doing it tough. The breakup of her marriage and worrying about money had both hardened and strengthened her. Sometimes though, he wished she wasn't so stubborn. No matter how many times he offered to help, she refused to accept anything from him, especially his money. It was a miracle she was letting him do the fencing. He steered the tractor towards the area of broken fencing. It was a long time since he'd done anything like this so hopefully he wouldn't stuff it up.

He was finishing up when his phone rang. Expecting it to be his mum, he didn't look at the screen as he answered.

'I'm almost done.'

'Jed?'

He froze. He didn't recognise the woman's voice. He'd changed phone numbers since retiring from footy, but occasionally a dogged journalist managed to track him down. Surely his story was old news now.

'Is that Jed?' the woman repeated.

He swapped the phone to his other ear. 'Yeah. This is Jed.'

'Hey. It's Zara.'

He exhaled in a rush and relief swept over him. 'Hi, Zara.'

'I hope you don't mind me calling. I rang your mum and she

gave me your number. She also gave me strict instructions not to give it out to anyone else.'

He chuckled. If he ever needed a bodyguard, Mum would be his first pick. 'All good. What can I do for you?'

'Listen, I was wondering if I could pop over and see you tonight.'

Cradling the phone between his ear and his shoulder, he dug his thumb into his lower back muscles. He'd forgotten how hard fencing was. 'Sure.' He didn't know what Zara wanted, but he had no reason not to see her. Over the years, they occasionally caught up whenever she was in Geelong. They'd have a drink and chat about old times. 'What time?'

'Does around six work for you?'

'Sounds good. I'll let Mum know you're coming.'

He disconnected the call and pocketed his phone. It would be good to catch up with Zara. Clearly, she and Georgie were still great friends so no doubt Zara would drop enough information about what Georgie was up to without him asking and raising anyone's suspicions.

He checked his watch, surprised by how late it was. He'd better get a move on so he could have a shower before Zara arrived.

Chapter 5

It was nearly six-thirty when Jed heard a vehicle pull up. He headed outside and stood on the veranda to greet Zara.

She climbed from her car and with a wave, headed over. 'Sorry I'm later than I said I'd be. My sisters are both expecting and Mum wanted to start talking about organising baby showers for them, then Dad had a meltdown because a delivery truck didn't show and now he's worried he won't have enough beer for the weekend. Then I had a call from work asking if I could come in—on a *weekend*. My boss wasn't impressed when I told her I was in Glengarrick. *Then* when I was unpacking my bag, I discovered I'd left my runners in Melbourne, so I had to make a mercy dash to Stockton to buy a new pair.' She let out an exaggerated groan. 'Of *course*, they didn't have my size, so I'll probably have massive blisters tomorrow.' She stopped to draw breath.

'Hi, Zara. Good to see you.' He held his arms open for a hug.

'Sorry.' She put her arms around his waist, squeezed once,

then dropped her hands. 'Sometimes I get on a roll and can't stop.'

He chuckled. Some things never changed. 'Come on in. Mum's looking forward to seeing you.'

'I hope she has the kettle on. I'd love a cuppa.' Zara jogged up the steps behind him and slipped off her boots, then padded behind him to the kitchen on socked feet.

He glanced at her. 'You sure you don't want something stronger. Beer? Wine?'

'You know what? A glass of wine sounds perfect. But just one. I'm driving.'

'And the last thing you need is to be hung over tomorrow for the run.'

'True, but it might take my mind off the impending blisters from my new shoes.'

'Mum, Zara's here,' he called out.

His mother popped her head out of the laundry and smiled before striding across the kitchen, arms wide. 'Hello, Zara darling. Lovely to see you. It's been far too long.' She gave Zara a hug. 'I swear you haven't changed a bit since school.'

'Hi, Michelle.' Zara laughed. 'I'm sure that's not true.'

'I've got a beef casserole in the crockpot if you're hungry.'

'Thanks, but I've already eaten. You know what Mum's like when all of us girls come home. I swear she thinks she's feeding the five thousand. I feel like every time I go back to Melbourne I have to put another hole in my belt.'

Michelle smiled. 'I heard your parents are going to be grandparents next year. Wonderful news. What about you? Any special man in your life?'

Zara shook her head.

If Jed hadn't been watching closely, he might have missed the faint tinge on her cheeks. He followed her on Instagram, and he'd seen photos of Zara with a woman called Kath. If he had to guess, Zara *did* have someone special in her life, but not a man.

'Oh, that's a shame. No one on the radar at least?'

'Definitely not a man, that's for sure.' Zara winked at him, confirming his suspicions.

'Well, I'll leave you two to catch up.'

Jed reached into the overhead cupboard and pulled out a glass, handed it to Zara, then opened a bottle of wine and poured it for her. Carrying their drinks, they headed back outside to the old church pew on the front veranda. Lilac-grey dusk settled over the land and crickets chirped.

'We couldn't have asked for better weather for the weekend,' he said.

'I love it up here this time of year. Nothing else quite like it.'

Shadows lengthened over the paddocks and for a while, only the croaking of frogs down at the dam broke the silence.

'Here's cheers to us.' Zara clinked her glass against his beer bottle before taking a healthy mouthful.

'Cheers,' he echoed. He took a swig of his beer, swallowed,

and exhaled slowly.

'I guess you're wondering why I wanted to see you.'

He smiled. 'Figured you'd tell me when you're ready.'

She took another sip of wine, swallowed, then leaned forward. 'I'm here about Georgie.'

He went still.

'I know you and I have never talked about that night, but I thought you should know Georgie's mum still doesn't know the truth about the accident.'

He nodded slowly. 'I wondered if she'd ever told her.'

'My parents don't know either.'

He took his time bringing the bottle to his lips and taking another mouthful of beer. He wasn't surprised neither Georgie nor Zara had told their parents the truth about the night of the storm. He hadn't breathed a word to anyone either. Ever. Nor would he.

They'd all had their reasons for keeping their secret. Zara hadn't wanted her parents to know she was gay. Georgie hadn't wanted anyone to find out she'd driven illegally, underage and without a license, and been the one to crash her best friend's car. He hadn't wanted anyone to find out he'd been knocked out by a tree. If he'd come clean at the time and admitted what happened, he wouldn't have been allowed to play football for two weeks which would have meant missing out on playing in the game the recruiters came to. Sharing the secret of that night might have changed the trajectory of his life.

Ten years on, he could see the decision not to say anything was the kind of decision three freaked out teenagers would make, but at the time, they'd all thought Georgie's plan would work. And clearly it had. As far as Jed knew, they were the only three people who knew what happened that night. Scratch that. Only he and Georgie knew what happened *after* he'd rescued her that night. His stomach knotted. They'd promised each other they'd never breathe a word to anyone, but maybe Georgie had said something to Zara and that's what Zara wanted to talk about.

'Georgie's mum's not in a good place.'

He snapped his head up. 'What do you mean?'

'Jane has severe depression. I mean really severe. She's barely left the house in years. That's why Georgie's stuck running the café.'

'I had no idea.'

Even though she'd been a bit off today, her smile seemed to indicate she was doing okay. But perhaps she was merely being polite.

Zara nodded. 'You know she studied nursing at uni?'

'Yeah.' He remembered at school she'd talked about becoming a nurse. 'That was always her dream.'

'She never graduated.'

Jed scrubbed a hand through his hair. What? He'd been living his best life and Georgie hadn't had a chance to follow her own dreams. That sucked. He silently cursed himself for being so self-centred and for not getting in touch with Georgie, or his friends, after he'd left town. Sure, he'd been busy at the club in those early days, but it wouldn't have been that hard to stay in contact with the people he'd gone to school with. And he definitely should have contacted Georgie after he heard her Dad died.

'You said Georgie's stuck running the café,' he said. 'Doesn't she want to? It looked to me like it was humming and she was in her element.'

Zara nodded. 'It is doing well. Don't get me wrong. Georgie's doing a superb job, but if you ask me, I think she's trapped here in Glengarrick.'

'And?' He knew Zara well enough to know she was hinting at something. 'What am I supposed to do about it?'

Zara gave him an "I'm glad you asked" look.

He sighed and waited.

'Georgie could use a friend.'

'I thought I already was her friend.' At least he hoped he still was.

'Georgie's forgotten how to have a good time. To let loose. And that's where you come in.'

'How? I don't see what Georgie's happiness has to do with me.'

After what he'd done by leaving town without talking to her and staying silent for ten years, it would be a miracle if she wanted to spend any time alone with him. Zara clearly hadn't noticed how awkward Georgie was around him earlier that day.

'I'm not saying you should be responsible for Georgie's happiness, but I've always felt there was something between you two.' Zara stared at him, unblinking. 'Something happened the night of the accident that changed her. Whenever I've asked her what went on between you two, she always denied anything happened. But I've often wondered.'

A trickle of sweat ran down his back. Maybe their secret was closer to the surface than either of them thought.

No wonder Zara was an excellent lawyer. She made him feel like he was sitting in the witness box under interrogation and she hadn't asked him one single question.

'Am I right?' Zara asked. 'Did something happen between you two that night?'

'Yeah, something happened, Zara. Georgie had a car accident—in *your* car—and I found her and rescued her. I'd say something big definitely happened,' he repeated.

He felt guilty for lying to Zara but keeping his word and keeping his and Georgie's secret was more important than anything.

Zara took her time sipping her wine, but her gaze never left his.

Thick silence fell between them.

'You know she was almost engaged,' she said finally.

He blinked. 'Who? Georgie?'

Zara nodded. 'The guy was a jerk. You should ask her about it.'

He'd love to ask Georgie about it because even after all these years she still pulled him in, but he didn't have the right to ask her anything personal. Intimate questions like that didn't feel right. At least not yet.

However, that didn't have to stop him asking Zara a question or two. Just to satisfy his curiosity, nothing more.

'Is she seeing anyone now?' he asked.

Zara grinned. 'Have you counted how many available eligible bachelors there are in Glengarrick our age?' She held up her hand forming a zero with her thumb and forefinger. 'And it's not like Georgie can leave town and find someone. Like I said. She's stuck because of the café.'

Zara had a point. Nearly all the kids left town as soon as they'd finished school, just as he and his friends had. Some returned, like Georgie. Most didn't. And as he'd figured earlier, anyone their age living in Glengarrick was probably already married.

'Rumour has it you're moving back permanently,' Zara said.

He'd been waiting for this question and it didn't surprise him. He'd figured stories would have flown the moment people found out he was coming back for the Grand Final.

'I'm still thinking about it. But the truth is, unless I can convince Mum to let me help her with the farm, there's probably not much point in staying. It's not like I have a job to come back to.'

'Do you need work?'

'Not straight away but I can't sit around the farm all day doing odd jobs and wondering if the place is ever going to be mine.'

Zara took another sip of wine before eying him over the rim of her glass again. 'So…back to Georgie.'

He exhaled softly. 'I recognise that look. You always were the schemer of the group.' Which was why it had surprised him when Georgie was the one to come up with the story to explain what happened on the night of the accident.

Zara chuckled.

He sat back on the pew and crossed his ankles. 'What are you thinking?'

'Tomorrow night after the run we're all getting together down at the creek to watch the fireworks.'

He nodded. 'I know. Charlie asked me to come.'

'I thought it would be really sweet if you packed a picnic and took a blanket and asked Georgie to sit with you.'

'Are you matchmaking?'

'Maybe.'

He chuckled.

'You have to admit, it would be romantic.'

'What happened to just being her friend?'

Zara smirked. 'I saw how you two looked into each other eyes today. Friends don't look at each other like that.'

'Get some glasses, Zazu. You saw nothing.'

She jumped up and set her empty wine glass on the pew. 'I'd better get going. I need to get a good night's sleep, or I'll be lucky to make it down the mountain in one piece tomorrow. Every year I tell myself to start training sooner than the week before the run, and every year I don't.' She put a hand on his shoulder. 'Don't get up.'

He raised his chin and tilted his head to receive the quick kiss Zara deposited on his cheek.

When she got to her car she stopped and turned around. 'Forgot to ask. Are you running in the morning too?'

'Yeah. I'll be there. I'm not a long-distance runner, but I've always wanted to come home and run the *Peak to Pub*. One of the things I hate about not playing is how much my fitness has dropped off, so it'll be good to stretch my legs. I won't be breaking any records though, that's for sure.'

'Lucky it's not a race, although tell that to Georgie.' She smiled. 'Righto, I'm off. We'll see you tomorrow.'

He waited for the noise of Zara's car to fade and the frogs to start up again before he went back inside.

He couldn't stop thinking about his little chat with Zara. A montage of images of Georgie popped into his head and his skin prickled. He knew sleep was likely to take a long time coming tonight so he flicked on the television and wasted hours watching home renovation shows. It was after eleven when Jed finally slipped between the sheets.

Staring up at the ceiling he listened as the old house creaked and shifted, then closed his eyes to shut out the vision of Georgie's lips on his. It might have been ten years, but he still recalled the way her warm body had felt next to his on that stormy night they'd never talked about since.

Chapter 6

Despite barely sleeping, Georgie felt energised when she woke before dawn on Saturday morning. At least this time, instead of her recurring nightmare, Jed had visited her dreams. She smiled again. They'd been good dreams.

Since surprising her yesterday when he'd walked into the café like no time had passed, she hadn't been able to get him out of her head. Thankfully after he left, the day got busier and no-one seemed to notice her mind was not on work.

Had he felt the same spark she'd felt, or had she imagined it?

'Are you wearing *makeup*?'

Georgie jumped and put a hand to her heart. 'Jeez, don't sneak up on me like that.'

Zara was leaning against the frame of the bathroom door with a smirk on her face.

'How long have you been standing there?' She'd been so lost in thought she hadn't heard the doorbell, let alone heard Zara come into the house. She finished applying mascara and ignored the looks Zara was shooting her way through the reflection in the mirror. 'I thought we were meeting at the pub. What are you doing here now?'

'I needed to get out.' Zara rolled her eyes. 'Honestly, the way Mum and Dad are acting, you'd think my sisters are the only women in Glengarrick to ever fall pregnant and I'm the only twenty-nine-year-old woman to still be single.'

Georgie laughed. Ian and Leanne were great, but they were conservative at heart and traditionalists when it came to their daughters. The fact Harriet and Lou were happily married with babies on the way was akin to winning the lottery for the Pritchards. That Zara was still single was something they couldn't get their heads around. No wonder Zara hadn't told her parents about Kath.

'Anyway,' Zara said, 'We're not talking about me. Why are you wearing makeup? You're going running, George, not on a date.'

'It's waterproof mascara,' Georgie said, as if that made any difference. She slipped the wand back into the tube.

'You've done your hair too.'

'I've *brushed* my hair.' Georgie pulled her long freshly straightened hair into its usual high ponytail. 'It's the first time in a year I've seen you guys. Call it an excuse to get dressed up. God knows there's no other reason to put makeup on in this town.'

Zara plopped down on the end of Georgie's unmade bed and

grinned. 'You sure there's not *one* reason for making yourself look cute? A certain sexy footballer by the name of Jed Delaney.'

'No!'

Georgie silently cursed her too quick response. Zara's grin morphed into a giggle and for a split-second Georgie was transported back to when they were tweens and use to sit cross-legged on Zara's bed, talking and giggling for hours about their secret crushes.

'Yeah, right,' Zara scoffed. 'I watched the way you acted when you saw him yesterday. You still have the hots for him, don't you?'

Georgie spun around and waved her hairbrush at Zara. 'You think I've got the hots for Jed? What are we? Thirteen? Jed is an old friend. Yours as much as he is mine.'

'I don't *think* you have a crush on him, I *know* you do. It's written all over your face.'

Heat flushed Georgie's cheeks. Zara was the only person who knew she'd spent the night of the storm at Jed's house, but Zara didn't know what had happened after he'd rescued her. Georgie glanced at Zara. Had she somehow put the pieces together and guessed?

She sighed. 'Let's say, yes, I think Jed's hot. After all, I have eyes and a heartbeat, but I'll make it clear. I'm not interested in doing anything about it.' She turned away from Zara and swept her makeup back into the drawer. Grabbing her running shoes from her wardrobe, she slipped them on and laced them up.

'I'm just saying,' Zara said, following Georgie down the hallway to the kitchen, 'you were quick to take Jed into your office before anyone else could get to him.'

'Oh, please,' she drawled, 'I was making sure he had some breathing room. If he'd stayed in the café, he'd have been inundated with people wanting selfies with him. You only had to take one look at his face. That was the last thing he would have wanted—people feeling sorry for him or making him out to be a hero.'

Zara's eyebrows rose. 'You seem to know an awful lot about what Jed wants. Especially since as far as I'm aware you haven't seen or spoken to him since he left.'

'You know as well as I do, Jed had a very good reason for leaving and since then he's understandably been focused on his career.'

'Hmmm. And now that career is over and he's back,' Zara said.

'I doubt he's here longer than the weekend.'

'Not what my sources say.'

Georgie filled up her drink bottle and slipped it into her backpack. As much as she didn't want to listen to town gossip, she wanted to know what Zara had heard. Georgie was tipping Zara knew exactly what Jed's plans were, but she wasn't going to ask more questions. That would be like raising a dozen red flags.

'I hear he's thinking about coming back for good.'

Georgie's heart sped. She glanced at Zara. 'And what's he going to do in Glengarrick? It's not as if the local footy team need a coach. They have Frank.'

'Don't ask me,' Zara said with a shrug. 'If you're so keen to know, you'll have to ask him yourself.'

'If I see him again and it's appropriate to ask, I will.'

'You need to move on from Neil.'

Georgie sighed loudly. 'Do we have to bring him into it?'

In third year of university, she'd been convinced Neil Monahan was "The One". She still remembered the day her dreams of a happy-ever-after ending with him came crashing down.

He'd been on the couch staring at the television when she'd arrived home from placement one afternoon. His dirty work boots were on the coffee table even though she'd told him dozens of times to leave his boots at the door. She'd leaned down and tried to give him a kiss, but when she got in the way of the TV screen, he shooed her away.

'How was your day?' she asked before she went into the kitchen in search of something to eat. She frowned at the unpacked shopping bags on the bench and pulled out a melted tub of her favourite ice cream. Couldn't he put away the groceries at least once?

'You hungry?' she called out from the kitchen.

When he didn't reply she'd stuck her head around the door to the living room. He hadn't moved from his position on the couch. Sucking in a deep breath she marched into the lounge room. Snatching the remote control from Neil's hands she pointed it at the television, muting the sound.

'Oi, what did you do that for?' he growled.

'We need to talk.'

'Can't it wait?'

She perched on the coffee table in front of him, stomach churning. 'No, it can't. Not this time.'

He met her stare and stared back like a petulant toddler. 'What?'

She stood, hands on hips and glared down at him. 'It's over.'

His eyes flicked from the muted television back to her. 'No, it's not. It's only half time.'

'It's a replay. You can watch it later. Anyway, I'm talking about us, not the football Us. This. This…whatever it is.' She lifted her hands and let them drop to her sides. 'I'm sick of *this*.'

'Jeez, George. Chill. Can't a bloke relax in his own house?'

A long stretch of silence filled the gap between them. He glanced behind her to the television obviously to check the score.

Georgie had enough. She crossed her arms over her chest. 'You need to leave.'

'What?'

'You heard me.'

'But—'

She raised both hands in the air like a shield to ward off the usual tsunami of excuses. She'd heard them all before.

Suddenly he leaned sideways, reached into the back pocket of his jeans, and pulled out a small black velvet box.

Even now she remembered how she'd felt the blood drain from her face. He'd never looked so serious and she'd never felt so sick. Had she made a monstrous mistake?

'Why now?' she asked, surprised how normal her voice sounded.

He jiggled the box in his hands. 'Is that a yes?' When she didn't reply, his lips thinned. 'Georgie?'

'No,' she whispered.

'No?' he echoed.

'I can't marry you. It would be a disaster.'

He stood and shoved the jewellery box into his pocket where it bulged like an ugly reminder of everything she was saying no to. 'Righto. I guess I'll go and pack up me stuff.'

Georgie opened her mouth to speak, but nothing came out. Seriously? He was giving up on her that easily?

He came out of the bedroom lugging his suitcase. 'If you change your mind, you can call me. I'll be at Jacko's place.'

She tried to swallow but her mouth was dry. 'I. . .no . . .'

Neil looked around the room, anywhere but at her. 'Righto. I'll come back tomorrow and grab the rest of my gear. If you can put it in some boxes and leave it out the front, I'll swing past after work.' He fiddled with his keys, sliding the key to her house off the metal ring. He tossed it on the coffee table. 'See you round.'

He walked out of the room and out of her life without a backward glance.

A week later her dad was diagnosed with cancer and when she called Neil and left him a message telling him, he didn't even have the decency to return her call.

After all these years the memories had almost faded, but Georgie had never been surer of anything that she'd made the right decision to leave him.

'Are you going to friend zone him?' Zara asked.

Zara's question brought Georgie back to the present. 'Who? What? No. It's not like Jed's shown any interest in me. We're friends. That's it. Now, come on, we'll be late.'

They walked down the hallway past the darkened front lounge room to the front door. The blinds were still down. Her mother was asleep on the couch, curled on her side with the blanket pulled up to her chin. The television was on mute in the background. Mum obviously hadn't gone to bed last night.

Hopefully when she woke, Mum would remember Georgie was doing the fun run.

'How is she doing?' Zara asked as Georgie pulled the front door softly closed behind them.

'Some days are worse than others.' Georgie unlocked her car

door with the key fob and glanced back at the house. 'Today is probably going to be one of those days.'

As Georgie followed Zara in her car back to the pub to catch the shuttle bus to the top of the mountain for the start of the run, she pushed aside her concerns for her mother's wellbeing. She'd had plenty of years to get used to her mum's fluctuating emotions. Worrying changed nothing.

***

An hour later, excitement hummed through Georgie's veins. As she and Zara got off the bus and headed for the start line in the upper car park, her heart gave a little one-two skip of anticipation. It was a bright, blue-skied morning, and even though it was still the middle of winter, the sun was warm, and the breeze had a fresh cut grass kind of tang to it.

'I can't believe you actually love doing this,' Zara said, stretching a quad muscle.

Georgie grinned. She hadn't always loved running. 'I vividly remember the day I woke, pulled on a pair of shorts and an old PE t-shirt from school, laced my runners, and took off. I only managed to jog for thirty seconds before I had to stop, calves screaming, lungs burning. I thought I was going to die.' After a quick rest to catch her breath, she'd started again, lumbering around the block for an incredible three minutes before she needed to stop again. 'I got home and collapsed after that first run and wondered when I'd gotten so unfit. Or if in fact I'd ever been fit at all.'

Zara laughed. 'That's how I feel every time I try to run.'

'I detested every moment of it, but I went back out the next day then the next until I started to enjoy it.'

'I don't think I'll ever enjoy it.'

'You would if you ran for an escape like I do. I love it. Best way I know to clear my head.' Barely a day went past that Georgie didn't run. 'I feel like my brain is always whirring, and running is the only way I know to switch it off. It helps me forget about Dad's death and Mum's illness. When I run, I don't think about anything except putting one foot in front of the other.'

'I can tell it's made a huge difference to your mental health.'

Georgie smiled. 'It has. I don't feel like I have that fog of depression over me anymore.'

'Do you ever regret leaving Melbourne after university to come back here to look after your dad?'

Georgie had been applying for Grad Year programs when her dad got sick with pancreatic cancer. There was never any question about what to do. She'd finished her final exam, put her career on hold and driven home the next day.

'Not at all. It gave me a chance to spend time with him. I loved taking him to his appointments then looking after him when he got sick. I guess you could say I put my newly minted nursing skills to the test and made sure he had the best care possible.'

She'd gladly looked after Dad until even his legendary positivity and stubbornness were no match for the cancer.

'I still don't get why you didn't leave and go back to Melbourne and try to get a job after he passed.'

Georgie shrugged. She'd considered doing that lots of times. 'I think something about nursing lost its appeal.'

'Or you lost your confidence.'

Georgie shrugged. 'Perhaps. Anyway, it wasn't like I could walk away from Mum. You know what happened after Dad died.'

'Yeah.'

'I couldn't leave her, and I couldn't leave everyone here. They were incredible the way they stepped in and helped, pulling together like we were one big family.'

The townsfolk were with Georgie and Jane through the worst of those awful days after Dad died and it hadn't felt right to walk away—almost like she'd be snubbing her nose at them if she left.

Zara chuckled. 'I'll bet you had more lasagne and casseroles in those six months your dad was sick than in your lifetime.'

'You'll notice there's no lasagne on the menu at the café.'

'Is your mum improving at all?'

Georgie shook her head. After Dad died, her mum's mental health plummeted. Georgie didn't speak about it often—partly because she didn't want the pity and partly because it wasn't her story to tell.

Her mother was diagnosed with severe clinical depression, but rather than follow the advice of her GP, Jane stopped leaving the house. That meant Georgie had no option but to step in and run the café as well as keep things going at home.

That first year, the thought of going back to Melbourne and picking up her nursing career didn't enter her mind. She stacked on weight and became depressed herself. Not that anyone knew. Mum was too far down her own dark hole, Dad was gone, and Georgie didn't want to confide in the local doctor—an older man who'd known her since she was a toddler. Instead, she worked long hours, operating on autopilot to keep the café open. Being busy at least stopped people from asking if she was okay.

'Mum attempted suicide last year, trying to overdose on some of Dad's leftover pain medication.'

Tears welled in Zara's eyes. She put an arm around Georgie's shoulders. 'Oh, honey, I didn't know it was that bad.'

'I kept it quiet. For Mum's sake.'

'Why does it sound like you're blaming yourself?'

'I should have gotten rid of his medication.'

'You weren't to know.'

'I knew.'

'I'll bet it must feel like everyone else's lives have continued and you're stuck here.'

'A little.'

It had been hard watching her friends from a distance as they started their new life chapters while she was back at home. But she wasn't one to complain. She got on with life and the café didn't skip a beat. She cracked jokes and remained social enough that no-one accused her of becoming a recluse like her mum. But in that first year she wasn't living. She was barely existing.

'I promise your turn will come one day,' Zara assured her, 'then you can stop pretending you're okay and start focusing on your dreams again.'

Georgie gave Zara a quick hug. 'Thank you. For everything.'

'I'm just glad you got the help you needed.'

Eighteen months after Dad passed, the grief and loss and everything she was dealing with at the café and with her mum compounded. She'd hit rock bottom and called Zara. Her friend had come home immediately, taken Georgie to Skipton to see a new GP who didn't know Georgie or her family history. With Zara's unwavering support—and anti-depressants—Georgie took up running.

After finishing her stretches, she jogged on the spot. 'Do you know if Jed's running today?' she asked, looking out over the crowd.

Zara nodded. 'Yep.'

'Do you think he's allowed to run? After his head injury?'

'No idea. I know as much as you do about Jed's retirement.'

Despite the amount of media coverage Jed's retirement had garnered, it seemed no-one in Glengarrick knew any more than what he'd told everyone at the press conference. After that night, he'd gone silent. He rarely posted on his social media accounts, but Georgie had checked them anyway, in the hope of gleaning new information. She'd learned nothing new.

'I'd guess he's not allowed to play contact sport again, but I'm sure running would be fine.' Zara nudged Georgie with her hip. 'That's another question you can ask him when you two catch up.'

Georgie ignored Zara's dig. 'Have you seen him yet?' she asked.

There were over five hundred runners registered for the run and they were gathered in the top car park ready to take off, having been shuttled up to the peak from the pub by bus. In a throng that size, Georgie didn't expect to see Jed, but she scanned the crowd anyway.

'No. But there are so many people here. It wouldn't be hard to miss him.'

'Are you kidding? The guy's a giant. He towers over every other human I know.'

Zara chuckled. 'Yeah, true.'

Georgie glanced at her watch. Less than ten minutes until the starter's gun. 'He'll have to get here soon, or he'll end up starting at the back of the pack.'

'He'll be here.'

'There he is!' She grabbed Zara's arm and pointed.

Jed was scanning the crowd too, and although Georgie didn't think he'd be looking for her, she lifted her hand and waved. When he caught sight of her, he smiled and waved back. A rush of pleasure went through her when he made a beeline for her.

The other runners, realising who it was, parted as if Jed were Moses and they were the Red Sea. As he passed, a few shook his hand or patted him on the back but despite how many people tried to stop him to chat, he still made it to Georgie's side with less than a minute to spare.

'Hey, guys, how's it going?'

He smiled at Georgie and Zara, but when his eyes grazed over her, lingering longer on her legs, the hairs on Georgie's arms prickled.

'Looking pretty fit, Georgie Porgie.'

Another warm flush spread over her body. She knew she looked good. Ten years ago, she hadn't been fat, but she'd lacked muscle tone.

'Thanks, Jed.'

He looked fit too, and despite trying to convince herself the sensation racing through her was her usual pre-race jitters, it wasn't. It was her hormones dancing, not adrenaline.

'Have you been training for this?' he asked.

'Ah, yeah, I suppose. I guess I have,' she stammered. Why couldn't she string two words together?

Zara laughed at her before turning to Jed. 'Mate! Wait 'til you see George run. You'll eat her dust.'

'As if,' Georgie said, rolling her eyes. She wasn't short, but

Jed was nearly forty centimetres taller than her and his legs came up to her waist. 'Look at his legs,' she added.

God knew she couldn't stop looking at them. His loose-fitting navy-blue training shorts did nothing to hide well-defined quads and toned calf muscles. Jed might have retired from professional football, but clearly, he hadn't stopped working out.

Jed chuckled. 'Trust me, these legs aren't made for long distance running.'

A siren sounded and the time for chatter ended. Putting her earbuds in, Georgie took off down the steep hill with a whoop, leaving Zara and Jed laughing behind her as they raced to catch up.

Chapter 7

On her way back home after the run, Georgie rolled down her car window and let the eucalyptus scent of the gum trees fill the car. She had run well—not her fastest time over twelve kilometres— but she was pleased she'd finished in the top ten women again this year. She was also secretly pleased to have beaten Jed. She'd waited for him at the finish line outside the pub and a rush of pleasure had swept through her when he'd congratulated her with a hug. His praise was genuine and the look on his face, one of surprise.

The bright morning sunlight bounced beams onto the black bitumen, and she smiled. During the run, clouds had moved up in the west and now they were splitting the sun into rays that splayed out in what Dad used to call the "fingers of God". For a second, she considered stopping to snap a photo, but there was no time, she needed to get home, shower, and go to work.

She'd left Abbey and Reece in charge of feeding the spectators and non-runners, but she'd promised to get back as soon as she could. Even though she'd put on two more staff to cater for the extra customers, the café would have been flat chat. Today they were only open until two; after that she'd head home and rest before heading down to the river. Zara had arranged for everyone to meet at six for drinks and an early picnic dinner while they waited for the fireworks. Jed had sidled up to her quietly after the run and told her he was looking forward to seeing her.

Glancing down at her speedo, she eased her foot off the accelerator. Whenever Georgie thought about Jed, shivers of excitement raced up and down her spine. The winding road was familiar, but the sun was blinding. Moments later, she hit something. Slamming her foot on the brake, her back tyres spun across the dirt edge before the car skidded to a stop. What was it? A koala or wombat? It couldn't have been a kangaroo because she would have seen it jump in front of the car. Whatever it was, it had felt like a lump of concrete.

Letting go of the steering wheel, Georgie straightened. As her heart rate settled, she unclipped her seat belt and opened the door, squinting as she walked around to the front of the car to see what she'd hit.

Her heart sank when she saw the crumpled body of a koala belly up on the road. Was it still alive?

She jogged over to it and crouched down, tentatively running her hands over the marsupial's soft fur. Her breath caught when a tiny black nose peered out of the pouch.

As she pulled out her phone to call wildlife rescue, another car pulled up behind hers. She lifted her head to see who it was and was surprised to see Jed get out of the Hilux.

He was by her side in two strides, his face ashen. 'Are you okay? What happened?'

'I'm fine. But I hit a koala.' She pointed. 'I think she's dead, but there's a baby in her pouch.'

He followed her to the front of her car and squatted beside the koala. Once he'd checked the mother was dead, he stripped off his hoodie, revealing a hint of toned abs when his T-shirt lifted.

'We need to keep it warm.' He gently removed the baby from the koala's pouch and cradled it close to his chest.

As she stood on the side of the road and watched him tenderly holding the koala, Georgie's stomach flipped. Jed hadn't changed. She remembered how compassionate and sensitive he'd been after her accident. As the adrenaline rushed through her, she shivered. She'd hit a koala and killed it, but she could easily have been run off the road and wrapped her car around a tree.

'I'll, ah…I'll call the wildlife rescue people,' she stammered, turning her attention to her phone, and looking for the number.

When she got through to them, she explained what had happened and where they were. 'Yeah, he's already wrapped it in his jumper to keep it warm,' she said. 'It's moving around so I think it's okay.'

'How big is it?' the man on the other end of the line asked.

She glanced at Jed. In his massive hands that could cradle a football with ease, the koala looked tiny. 'It looks like one of those little stuffed toys they sell at the airport. It would easily fit in my cupped hands.'

'Someone will be there in about ten minutes.'

'Thanks.' She disconnected the call and moved closer to Jed.

'The guy on the phone said you did the right thing wrapping it up so quickly,' she said, trying to focus on the koala snuggled against Jed's chest, not the size of his flexed biceps. 'He said we need to keep it quiet and warm. He'll be about ten minutes.'

Jed stroked its head. 'I was chatting to someone today and they were saying the drought's caused a lot of problems for the koalas. The drier it gets, the scarcer food becomes, and they're drawn closer to the road where the gum trees grow.'

She murmured her agreement, but she wasn't listening. She was fixated on his tanned hands.

'Georgie?'

'Huh? Sorry. What did you say?'

A frown creased his brow. 'Are you okay?' he asked.

'I'm fine. A little shaken up.' And not simply because she'd hit the koala. Being this close to Jed was doing all sorts of weird things to her nerve endings, as if her body were waking up from a coma.

The koala had fallen asleep, wrapped in Jed's jumper, cradled against his chest. He moved back to his car and Georgie followed him. When he leaned against the bonnet, she copied him, leaning close and touched the bundle in his hands.

'It's so small,' she said. 'I feel so bad for killing its mother.'

'These things happen, Georgie. At least you stopped. Plenty of people would have kept driving.'

'I couldn't do that.'

'You always had the softest heart,' he said, speaking softly so as not to disturb the koala.

Her pulse quickened. 'Thank you.'

After a beat, Jed shifted slightly so he could face her. 'You ran well today. You're good. Fast. I don't remember you running at school. If I remember, you played netball.'

'I did play netball. Not well. I started running not long after Dad died.'

'And you clearly love it.''

She nodded. 'I do. After Dad passed, Mum struggled and rather than me fall apart too, I took up running. To be honest, it was to prove to everyone that I was fine. I wasn't, but the more I ran, the easier things got and the more I fell in love with running. When I run it's like I'm no longer in the driver's seat. All I can think about is the burn in my legs, the swing of my arms, my heart rate, and the rhythm of my breathing. It's the best feeling.'

'I totally get that.' His face took on a contemplative expression for a second before a frown creased his brow. 'I feel so bad, Georgie. I had no clue things were so tough for you after your dad died.'

'Yeah. Very tough. But everyone's been great—I couldn't ask for a more supportive community than the people in Glengarrick.'

'I really should have gotten in touch.'

'You had your own battles.'

His face hardened for a second before relaxing. 'Yeah, I guess.'

Confiding in Jed felt so natural, like she'd slipped on her most comfortable jumper. Usually when she talked to anyone about her dad, she did so with a tightness in her throat and tears close to the surface. But the way Jed listened and seemed to understand didn't make her feel as vulnerable or afraid.

'How's *your* mum doing?' she asked carefully, aware that Jed might feel uncomfortable sharing his own feelings with her.

Jed's mum didn't venture off the farm often and when she did come into town, she kept to herself. The divorce and the gambling had not been private. Georgie wondered if Michelle did her grocery shopping in Stockton to avoid bumping into people. She couldn't remember the last time she'd seen Jed's mum in town.

'She's good. Really well actually…considering. She's one of the toughest women I know.'

'Do you have any contact with your dad?'

He shook his head and in that one tiny move, she sensed his pain. 'I'm sorry about what happened to *your* family, Jed. I could have contacted you, too.'

'I guess neither of us expected life to turn out the way it has.'

That was an understatement. She couldn't help but admire his bravery for talking about his own painful experiences.

'You must miss playing football,' she said.

He stroked the koala's head and when he didn't say anything for a long moment, she regretted asking such a personal question. Opening herself up to Jed had made her feel closer than ever to him, but he might not feel the same way. He might regret confiding in her.

'I miss it more than I can explain,' he said finally without looking up.

She let a long beat of silence sit between them.

'Did you have to retire?' She only knew as much as she'd heard in the press conference so perhaps there was more to the story.

He lifted his head and met her gaze. 'Yeah. I consulted three independent neuro-specialists and they all came back with the same conclusion. I had no choice. According to the doctors, I'll be far more susceptible to any little head knock going forward and my recovery time from any knock would be lengthened. They said it's not worth the risk. It was an untenable position to be in, both in terms of my football career and my health.'

His voice was flat, like a deflated balloon and her heart broke for him. Guilt flickered. This wasn't the kind of conversation they should be having on the side of the road. He was evidently struggling to maintain his composure and clearly, she'd touched a nerve. She was about to change the subject when he reached out and put a hand on her arm.

'Sorry, George. I still get pretty emotional about it.'

'That's okay. You're allowed to. I'm sure it's still raw.'

He took his hand away and stroked the koala again. 'It's the finality of it that gets me. That I'm not going to be able to play with the boys and experience that level of mateship ever again. I never thought it was something I'd have to face so soon. I hoped I'd get to play at least another five years.'

'I watched that game when you got knocked out the first time earlier this season.'

He grimaced. 'Mum says she still has nightmares about it.'

'It was awful. I was at work. No-one said a word until you were on that stretcher and gave a thumbs up.'

'I have no recollection of any of it.'

'If I remember, you took two weeks off.'

'I did. I couldn't think straight and had debilitating headaches, but I didn't tell anyone. I couldn't remember things and I couldn't exercise because I felt like garbage. I realised things were bad when I was heading to training one night and I got to an intersection without knowing how to get to the ground despite the fact I drove the same route every time. I had to call the coach and admit I was lost.'

'That must have been really scary.'

'The coaches were worried, but I had to act like it was no big deal.'

'Then you had the second knock.'

'There were a few in between that too.' He shrugged. 'It's one of those flukes that happen sometimes in footy.'

'So, no more contact sport.'

'That's right.'

A van pulled up behind Jed's car, putting an end to their conversation.

'Looks like this little guy's rescuer is here.' Jed pushed himself off the front of his car and carried the koala to the man walking towards them.

The guys eyes widened when he recognised Jed. He extended his right hand. 'Hi. I'm Gary.'

'G'day,' Jed said, shaking Gary's hand before handing over the tiny bundle.

They chatted while Gary slipped the koala into a little pouch he'd brought with him. He offered Jed his hoodie back.

'It's all good. Keep it.'

Gary's eyes widened further. The jumper was a Cats hoodie—not one that could be bought in a store. 'Thanks, mate. My son won't believe me when I tell him I met you.'

'He likes footy?' Jed asked.

'Loves it. He's barracked for Geelong ever since he knew you grew up here.'

'How old is he?'

'Eight.'

'Give me a second.' Jed jogged back to his car and returned a moment later with a black sharpie. 'What's your son's name?'

'Mason.'

Reaching over, Jed scribbled Mason's name then signed his own on the back of the hoodie.

'That's awesome.' Gary beamed at him. 'Thanks so much. He'll love it.'

'No worries. Look after this little guy too,' Jed said, stroking the koala's soft fur again.

Georgie watched the interaction with interest. Jed's fame obviously hadn't gone to his head. She'd presumed he'd have an ego, but from what she'd seen of him so far, he was incredibly humble. No wonder he had such a great reputation both on and off the field. Regardless of how much he was still reeling from the loss of his career and his future, he managed to smile and make someone else's day. How many people could do that?

She could learn a lot from him.

After Gary left, she checked her watch. *Crap. Look at the time!*

'I'd better get going. Reece and Abbey will be wondering where I am.'

He raised his eyebrows in question, searching her face.

'Work. It's one of our busiest days of the year.'

'Of course.'

She gave him a quick hug. 'Thanks for stopping and helping me out. You have such a big heart. Because of you, that little koala will probably make it.'

She turned away, but Jed caught her arm and pulled her back to him. He tapped her heart with his fingers. 'No, Georgie. *You* have a big heart. There's something special in there.'

Even after he stepped away, she felt the lingering warmth of his hand where he'd touched her. 'Thank you, Jed.'

That light touch reminded her of the last time he'd trailed his fingers over her skin. Heat roared up her neck to her cheeks and she turned away and headed for her car, hoping he couldn't read her mind or see how red her face was.

She paused before getting in the car. 'I'll still see you tonight. For the fireworks,' she added, in case he'd forgotten.

'I'll be there.'

'We usually sit at one of the picnic tables under the peppercorn tree.'

'Save me a seat.'

As she drove away, she couldn't stop the grin forming.

Chapter 8

Jed watched Georgie's little red car until it was out of sight. The morning sun filtering through the trees had made her brown hair look as though it was streaked with gold and it had taken all his strength not to run his fingers through it. Whenever he was near her, the tightening in his gut confirmed it: he was still attracted to her. But did Georgie feel the same?

When he'd seen her car parked crookedly on the side of the road, his heart had gone into overdrive. His first thought was she'd been in an accident. As he'd pulled over, memories of the night of the storm flashed in front of his eyes. He'd raced over to her and when she'd looked up at him with tears in her hazel eyes, all he'd wanted to do was take her in his arms and smooth away whatever was bringing her pain.

Once he knew she was okay, relief had flooded him, and his heart rate had returned to a steady beat. She was safe. And so was the koala.

Jed slid behind the wheel and started the key. Stopping had delayed his plans to have a chat with his mum, but he didn't mind.

He'd possibly saved the koala's life which was good. And he'd got to spend more time with Georgie which was even better. The elephant in the room was still between them, but at least she was talking to him. Hopefully, later tonight, at the fireworks, he'd have a chance to get her alone so he could say sorry for leaving town after he was drafted and for not staying in touch. His apology was long overdue.

When he got home, Mum was on the pew on the front veranda enjoying the morning sun. She had a coffee mug in hand and her laptop on her knees. She looked up as he pulled up.

He took his time getting out of the car. Was now a good time to try to have another conversation with Mum?

'How was the run?' Mum asked.

'It was good. Lots of people. Well organised.'

Mum patted the spot beside her as she closed the lid on her laptop. He sat and draped his arm over the back of the pew. 'What are you doing?' He pointed to the computer.

She shrugged. 'Just looking over the budget.'

He exhaled slowly.

'Mum—'

She rested a hand on his knee. 'I don't want a handout, darling.'

He twisted to face her. 'Why do you have to see it as a handout, Mum? Would it make you feel better if I gave you a loan?' He'd put the offer on the table, even though there was no way he'd ever let her pay him back. 'I had no idea how rundown the place is'

It was Mum's turn to sigh. 'I didn't want you to know.'

'Why? Is there a reason you don't want me to help?'

'I don't want you to be stuck with the farm once I'm gone.'

He frowned. 'You don't want me to take over from you?' They'd never talked succession planning, but he'd always assumed he'd take over the farm when Mum couldn't do it on her own anymore.

'I don't want you to unless this is what you really want. Farming isn't something you do part time.'

'I know.'

Silence fell.

'What do you want to do?' Mum asked after a while.

'I'm not entirely sure, but I was hoping you'd let me come home until I work it out. I've asked my agent to put out some feelers. He said there might be a job going at a club in Melbourne for an assistant coach but I'm not confident.'

'What about player welfare at Geelong? Is there a role there?'

He shook his head. 'I'd love to, but they already have someone and he's great.'

'Do you miss playing, darling?'

'Yeah. A lot. But mostly I just miss being around the club. Being with the boys. Training, that sort of thing.'

'Then why don't you see what your agent says? If nothing

comes of the assistant coaching job, then we can talk about you taking over the farm.'

'That sounds like a good idea.'

Mum stood. 'Work doesn't get done if I sit around all day.'

'Is there anything I can help you with?'

She opened her arms for a hug. 'You already have, darling, you already have.'

***

After spending the rest of the morning helping weed the veggie garden, Jed had an early lunch then headed back into town to buy groceries. On his way back from the supermarket, he drove down the main street and spotted a line of people standing outside the Silver Spoon. He frowned. What were they waiting for? Georgie said she'd be snowed under, but he hadn't expected to see people queuing around the corner.

Curious to know what was going on, he made a split-second decision and pulled into a vacant car space. He entered the café and spotted Georgie immediately. He stood in the doorway for a moment, watching without her noticing him.

Yesterday she'd looked busy, but not rattled. Today her cheeks were flushed, and stray wisps of her hair had escaped from her ponytail.

As if sensing someone was watching her, she glanced up. As

he walked towards her, the frown became a smile, but she still looked flustered.

'Hope you're happy to wait awhile,' she said.

'It's busy,' he said, stating the obvious.

'Crazy. One of the extra casuals I put on for this weekend called in sick with gastro. If I'd known, I wouldn't have run this morning.'

'Damn.'

'I rang Zara, but she's helping her parents out at the pub. They're slammed too and taking our overflow.'

'What about your mum? Could she come and help?'

A fleeting shadow moved across Georgie's face and if he hadn't been watching her so closely, he would have missed it. Realising what he'd said, he immediately regretted his question.

The phone started ringing and he reached for it, grabbing it before she did. 'Silver Spoon Café, how can I help you?'

'Jed! What are you doing?'

He winked.

She put her hands on her hips and glared at him, but he could tell she wasn't really upset. He poked out his tongue, turned his back and took the order. After hanging up, he turned back to face her. 'Have you eaten?' It was one-thirty and he'd spotted a half-drunk coffee on the counter beside an uneaten sandwich.

She tightened her ponytail. 'I haven't had time to eat.'

'There's always time for food. Go. And drink some water too.'

'I can't. Have you seen how many people are waiting outside? I've never known it to be like this. I was wondering if news got around yesterday that you might do a reappearance.'

He chuckled. 'I'm not that famous.'

'You are in Glengarrick.'

Spotting an apron hanging from a hook, he grabbed it, putting it over his head and tying it behind his back.

Georgie's eyes widened. 'What are you doing now?'

'Helping you.' He picked up the plate with the sandwich and put it in her hands before gently shoving her in the direction of the kitchen. 'Take a break, George. You'll do no one any good if you pass out. And while you're out there eating, take a few deep breaths.'

'Jed.'

'Don't argue,' he warned with a grin.

'But I'm the one in charge here.'

'Not for the next five minutes you're not.' He turned his back on her and smiled. 'Now, who ordered the chicken burger?'

'I did.' A tween at a table of four waved her hand in the air. When he placed the plate carefully in front of her, she batted her lashes at him. 'Hi, Jed.'

'G'day, how's it going'?'

'Who knew we'd be having our lunch served by a legend,' the girl's dad said.

Jed smiled as he put the man's order in front of him. 'Don't know about that. It's a team game.'

'Would it be too much to ask for a photo?' the girl's mother asked. She put an arm around a young boy next to her and beamed at Jed. 'Ollie's followed your career since he was old enough to hold a football.'

'No worries.' Jed grabbed the woman's phone and held it up for a selfie, making sure the whole family were in the picture. After handing it back, he tipped his cap and went back to the counter where Georgie stood, staring at him, with laugher in her eyes.

'If you stop to take photos with everyone, word will get out and you'll only have more people to serve.'

He chuckled. 'I don't mind, and it'll be good for business.'

'Are you sure you don't mind helping?'

'Not at all. Now *go*. I have food to take out.' He slipped past her and grabbed two more plates from the servery window. 'Which table?' he asked Abbey.

Ten minutes later, Jed wondered how Georgie managed to keep up with the pace. Abbey and the other staff had him running as they handed him coffee and food orders. It all became a blur and when the lunch rush ended, he was grateful when Abbey said he could turn the "open" sign to "closed".

As Jed pulled out a stool and sat, Georgie grabbed a broom. She was about to start sweeping when Zara walked in.

Jed held up a hand. 'We're closed, Zazu. You'll have to come back tomorrow.'

'Bite me. I need a coffee.'

'Don't you have a coffee machine at the pub?' he replied.

Zara rolled her eyes. 'You're kidding, right? You'd let Dad make you a coffee? I swear instant coffee is better than what he could make. It cracks me up that he calls himself a barista just because he did a one day online course.'

Abbey giggled. 'I'll make you one, Zara. Anyone else want one before I turn the machine off for the day?'

'Large double shot for me please, Abbey,' Jed said. 'Hey, Purcell,' he called out to Georgie. 'It's fulltime. Siren's gone. You can stop playing now.'

She laughed but kept straightening the furniture. 'Did we win?'

'I'd reckon. Lots of happy customers today.'

'How many selfies did you take?' she asked.

It was his turn to laugh. He didn't need the fuss, but it came with the role so he'd obliged every thrust of a pen or phone in his direction figuring it wouldn't hurt Georgie's business or his reputation.

He was in awe of Georgie. She'd run around like the Energiser bunny and her smile never faltered. Meanwhile, he was pooped. 'Wish I'd worn my GPS tracker. I reckon I did more kilometres today than I do on the field.'

'I wore my Fitbit once. I did well over eleven thousand steps in a day,' Abbey said.

When Georgie disappeared into the back, Jed turned to Zara. 'Does she ever slow down?'

'Not that I've seen,' Zara replied. 'She's afraid to.'

'Afraid of what?'

'Of what she might find out about herself if she stops.'

Jed frowned. 'What do you mean?'

'Once she stops going a mile a minute, she'll realise she's forgotten how to dream.'

After Abbey made their coffees, Zara left with hers in a keep cup and Abbey switched off the coffee machine and started cleaning it.

Jed found Georgie in the office and dragged her out by the hand. 'Georgie, stop. Come and sit with me.'

She stretched her arms above her head to ease the kinks in her back before pulling out a stool and sitting. 'I don't even know what to say, Jed. I just…you just…' Her words trailed off. 'Thank you.'

'It's no big deal.'

'Maybe not to you.'

Jed glanced up at the clock above the counter. 'What time do you have to head down the river?'

'Around six.'

'You should go home and take a nap.'

'I might.' She pulled the band from her ponytail and fluffed out her hair, letting it fall loose around her shoulders. In the late afternoon light coming through the café windows, it picked up the caramel highlights again.

They chatted for a while until Abbey had finished. With a wave she closed the door behind her and left them alone.

'Are you staying in town for long, Jed?'

'Why? Are you looking for staff?'

She chuckled. 'Maybe.'

'I don't know. Mum and I were just talking about it this morning. I'm waiting to hear from my agent.'

She shifted position on the stool. 'Agent? I thought you'd retired. You're not planning to play for another club?'

He shook his head. 'No. My agent can help find me non-playing roles too.'

'Oh. Like in the media?'

'Definitely no!' He chuckled. 'I'm not cut out for commentating. I'd be too opinionated.'

'What about coaching?'

'Exploring the possibilities.' He didn't want to say too much in case it didn't come off. He also wasn't sure why he didn't want to say anything to Georgie about the possibility of staying in Glengarrick on the farm if the assistant coaching role didn't come off.

'Do you want to coach?' she asked.

'I don't know. To be honest, I'd never given much thought to what life looked like after playing. If I don't take a role in football,

I'm not sure what other options I have.'

She frowned. 'Didn't you study sports science at university?'

He looked at her and noted the blush on her cheeks.

'I remember reading that somewhere,' she said in a rush.

'I have a degree, but I've never used it.'

'Like me,' she said, dipping her head. Slipping off the stool, she removed her apron. 'Time to head home.' She moved away from him and flicked off lights and pulled down the blinds. 'Thanks for all your help today, Jed.'

'You're welcome.' He didn't like that their conversation was ending on an awkward note. 'I'm really looking forward to tonight.'

She stopped and turned to face him. A fleeting smile crossed her face. 'So am I.'

Chapter 9

Ten Years Earlier

Georgie woke to total darkness. Gale force squalls lashed the trees around her and over the sound of the rain on the roof of the car, she heard the branches of the river gums creaking and groaning as they were whipped wildly in the wind. Her head hurt and when she touched it, her fingers came away covered in warm, sticky blood. She tried to take a deep breath but the pain in her ribs was so bad, black spots formed before her eyes.

She grappled with the steering wheel airbag to get it out of the way, but the movement and change in position caused the car to shudder and sigh like the cry of a wounded animal. She took a deep breath and slowly shifted position but even that was too much. The car dropped like a rollercoaster carriage before coming to rest with a jerk.

It took ten long seconds for her breathing to steady.

Slowly and deliberately, she moved her legs first, then her arms, to see if she'd broken anything. She exhaled in relief when everything seemed to work okay. Other than the gash to her head and the pain in her ribs, from what she could tell, she was miraculously unhurt.

She stared out through the shattered windscreen. She might be okay, but from what she could see of the crumpled bonnet in front of her, Zara's car wasn't. Resting against the broken guardrail, it was tilted at a precarious angle, nose first. A massive gum tree on the driver's side pinned her door closed and the passenger side window had exploded on impact.

She unclipped her seatbelt, but even that tiny movement was too much. She screamed when the car lurched forward, dropping with another sickening jolt and moan and causing the pain in her ribs to intensify.

Outside the car, muddy water swirled as the creek rose. A shiver ran through her. How much longer before the car started to fill with water? If she didn't get out, she could drown or be swept away with the car down the creek. Another gust of wind howled and whined and burning tears formed. She closed her eyes and fought the rising fear. If she didn't get out, she could die.

'Help!' she wailed. Her voice was carried away by the wind, but she shouted again anyway. 'Help!'

From where the car had rested in the gully, even if someone drove past, they wouldn't see her. They might notice the missing guardrail, but in this weather, they probably wouldn't think much of it. They'd be focussed on getting home. From what she could tell, there was no sign of the other car that had hit her either.

The tears turned to sobs and her chest became so tight she could barely breath.

She wasn't sure whether she was having a panic attack, or if she'd punctured a lung. Hopefully the former, but the latter was serious. Taking a few shallow breaths, she counted to five then exhaled slowly. The pain didn't decrease, but it didn't get any worse either.

She silently cursed her decision to take the back roads from Stockton to be safe. The only people who used this road were locals, and most sensible locals would be safely tucked up at home. Which was where she wanted to be. She had to get out of the car because it could be hours before someone came past.

She lifted her head at a sound. Was someone yelling, or was it the wind playing tricks on her?

'Zara! Zazu!'

Not the wind. 'Help,' she shouted. 'Help me!'

'Hold on. Don't move. I'm coming down.'

Relief swept through her. *Thank you, God*.

Her rescuer peered down from the top of the gully. His body was backlit by the headlights of a car and she couldn't make out who it was, but she didn't care. She was going to be alright.

'Are you okay, Zara?' The man shouted.

'It's Georgie,' she called back. 'Georgina Purcell.'

'Is Zara okay too?'

'It's just me,' she cried out. Naturally whoever it was would assume they were both in the car, and in the darkness, he probably couldn't see Georgie was the one behind the wheel. She had a lot of explaining to do.

'Are you hurt?'

His voice was closer, and Georgie turned her head to the left and watched whoever it was sliding down the gully towards her. Her eyes widened when he got closer and she saw who it was.

Jed.

'Can you move, Georgie?'

His voice was steady and confident, and it had an oddly calming effect on her. She drew in a shuddering shallow breath and winced at the pain again. 'I…I think so.'

He peered into the car through the broken passenger side window. 'You're bleeding.'

'I hit my head and my chest hurts, but I'm okay. I think,' she added. For all she knew she'd damaged internal organs and was bleeding to death. 'No broken bones from what I can tell, and I can move my legs so I'm not pinned in.'

His eyes darted left then right. She was beyond grateful he didn't ask why she was driving Zara's car. He knew she didn't have her license yet.

'We need to get you out of there.'

You think? 'I'm too scared to move.'

'Fair enough. From what I can see, the guardrail is the only thing holding up the car. If it snaps, you'll end up in the creek.'

'Pretty sure I'm already in the creek. Shit creek.' Her attempt at humour fell flat and she started to cry again.

'You're going to be okay, Georgie.' Jed reached through the car and touched her arm, giving it a squeeze. 'If you can move towards me, I should be able to pull you through this window. I can't promise it won't hurt, but I don't see any other way of getting you out quickly. This car could go any minute.'

'Can't you open that door?'

'There's a tree branch pinning this one shut too. If you want, you can wait while I go for help.' He glanced back up at the road then back at her. 'It could be awhile.'

She shook her head so hard it felt like her brain bounced. 'No.' She wanted to get out of there now. Then she could work out how to fix this mess.

Dark brown eyes stared into hers. 'You're going to be fine. I promise. I won't let you get hurt. You just need to trust me okay?'

She swallowed past the lump in her throat and nodded. 'Okay. But I'm going to be in so much trouble.'

'Don't think about that now. Let's get you out first.' He backed away from the car. 'Give me a second. I've got a tarp in my boot. I'll grab that and cover the broken glass, so you don't hurt yourself when I pull you out.'

He disappeared into the darkness and while she waited, Georgie tried not to cry. Her parents would be expecting her home any minute and if she didn't arrive home or at least contact them, they'd be on the phone to the police and arranging a search party. How was she going to explain what she was doing driving Zara's car without dobbing Zara in and getting her into more trouble? And the bigger issue was how was she going to explain why Zara's car was a total wreck at the bottom of the creek? No matter what happened, she was going to be in a world of trouble, and so was Zara.

Miraculously, her phone was still resting in the cupholder on the dash. She tucked it into her bra, noticing there was a missed call from Zara. She'd deal with that later. Thankfully no messages from Mum.

When Jed returned, after an agonisingly long time, he was carrying a plastic tarp and a navy hoodie. His hair was plastered to his head and his clothes were soaked through. After he wrapped the jumper around his waist, he took a moment to position the tarp over the broken glass.

'Let's get you out of there.'

'Can you reach my bag?' she asked. She could see it on the passenger side floor where muddy water was starting to pool but she couldn't reach it without making the car move again.

Jed carefully reached in, grabbed her bag and tossed it in the direction of the road before wrapping his hands gently around her wrists and closing his fingers over them. 'You're going to be fine, okay? I'll count to three and pull you out. Trust me. I won't let you go. Promise.'

She nodded, not taking her eyes off his face. His brow creased in concentration, but she saw no sign of fear in his eyes and that instilled a mustard seed of faith within her. 'Okay. Let's do this.'

'On three.'

She braced herself.

'One…two…three!'

With superhuman force, Jed pulled her out of the car, and she collapsed on top of him on the muddy embankment. Seconds later, with a screech of metal, the guardrail gave way and Zara's car tumbled nose-first down the last few metres of the gully, before landing in the raging water. They stood and stared at it, neither of them speaking as rain fell on them.

When she started shivering uncontrollably, Jed pulled her close and pressed a tender kiss to the top of her head. 'It's okay, you're okay,' he whispered.

She was far from okay, but his calm words had a soothing effect on her.

'You must be freezing.'

She nodded. Her bare arms were covered in goose bumps and she rubbed at them, shuddering again, partly from the cold and partly from the shock. She felt like throwing up. If Jed hadn't driven past, she'd be with the car, swept down the creek.

Jed released her and unwrapped his hoodie from around his waist. He gently tugged it down over her head then helped her put her arms in the sleeves. It swam on her, but she was instantly warm and dry. He pulled her against his chest again and she melted into his embrace, inhaling the scent of his deodorant and aftershave as violent sobs racked her body again.

It took a long time to get herself together and when she wiped the tears from her eyes her hands come away red.

Jed stared at her hands then her head and swore softly. 'That wound looks nasty. We need to get you to hospital.'

She pushed away from him, wincing in pain as she stumbled on the uneven ground. The reality of her situation snapped her back to the present. Now wasn't the time to think about her secret crush on Jed Delaney.

'No! I need to get home.'

Illuminated by the headlights from his car, his face was ashen. 'Your head's bleeding pretty bad, Georgie. I should take you to the hospital to get you looked at. And I don't like the way you're holding onto your side.'

She shook her head again, causing a trickle of fresh blood to snake down the side of her head. 'I have to get home,' she repeated. 'Mum and Dad will be going nuts worrying about me.'

'If your goal is to *not* panic your parents, I don't recommend you walk in the door looking like that.'

She touched her head again and her fingers found fresh blood. 'What am I going to do?' she asked, voice wobbling.

'Can you call your mum and tell her you're staying the night at Zara's?'

'No. Zara's parents think she's staying at mine.'

'Where *is* Zara?'

She hesitated. She'd promised Zara she would cover for her, no matter what. 'In Stockton. With a…a friend.'

Jed raised his eyebrows but thankfully didn't ask any more questions.

'You could always stay at my place, I guess. My parents are away for the weekend. Call your mum, tell her you're safe and staying at Zara's. I'll cover for you.'

The guy was a hero and a saint. One day she would thank him.

'What will I do about the car?' she asked, gazing down the gully.

He shrugged. 'We'll figure something out. Let's get you warm first.'

He helped her up the last few metres of the embankment to his car. The rain had eased slightly, but the wind hadn't. They both heard the crack at the same time.

Georgie jumped left while Jed dove right, and the branch crashed down between them.

After catching her breath, Georgie struggled to stand. There was no sign of Jed. She got to her feet and scanned the road as she called for him, but the wind picked up her voice and carried it away.

When she finally spotted him, her heart leapt to her mouth. Screaming his name, she scrambled back down the slippery embankment until she reached him.

He wasn't moving.

Chapter 10

Hands reached down and grabbed her arms, yanking and pulling her from the car with such force it took what was left of her breath away.

Georgie shot up, gasping, before laying back and closing her eyes, waiting for her breathing to settle. She never had the nightmare during the day. Throwing the pillow to the end of the bed, she tossed aside the twisted doona and knuckled the sleep from her eyes. She probably shouldn't have taken a day time nap, but she wanted to hang out with everyone tonight and stay awake for the fireworks, so she'd taken Jed's advice in the hope some sleep would give her a second wind.

After a quick shower to wake herself up, she applied some makeup and did her hair, knowing that Zara would notice and probably say something again. She opened the curtains and was disappointed to see that while she'd napped, the nice weather had turned nasty. The sky was now a sullen grey and dark clouds skittered by, blown by a strong southerly breeze.

She stood at the window for a moment, gazing out across the paddocks beyond their back yard. She loved living in this house. After Dad died, her mum couldn't handle the memories of their old place, so Georgie had encouraged her to buy this house. It backed onto parkland, then flat paddocks flanked by bushland and the mountains beyond that. It was such a peaceful spot.

She heard movement in the kitchen and smiled. She didn't expect her mum would go to the fireworks, but if she was up and about, that was a good sign.

'Hey. How're you feeling?' Georgie asked carefully as she entered the kitchen. Depending on the day, that simple question could spark off a tsunami of tears or an avalanche of anger. Mum's moods were so volatile.

'I'm okay, thanks.'

Georgie put on a smile. *"I'm okay thanks."* That was basically Mum's stock answer since Dad died.

In Georgie's opinion, Mum was living the furthest from *okay* that anyone could live.

'I'm heading off to the fireworks. Zara and the rest of the school crew will be there. Why don't you join us? Even Jed Delaney's back in town.' Mum had always been a Jed fan.

'Not this time.'

Georgie knew enough to back off. She pecked her mother's cheek. 'I'd better get going. They'll be wondering where I've gotten to.' With a wave, she scooted out the front door.

When she got to the river, she headed straight for the picnic table under the peppercorn tree where Zara and the others sat, huddled in puffer jackets, beanies, and scarves. There was no sign of Jed.

'Hey,' she said when she got closer. 'How cold is it?' She stamped her feet and rubbed her gloved hands together.

Kate made room for Georgie at the table.

'If this wind keeps up, they'll have to cancel the fireworks,' Ben said.

'I reckon it'll clear up,' Jack said, ever the optimist.

For the next couple of minutes, they chatted about the forecast while checking the weather apps on their phones. It didn't look like clearing which was such a shame. If there was too much wind, they wouldn't let off the fireworks.

'Hey, Georgie, heard you got yourself a hot new staff member at the café,' Kate said.

Georgie's heart hammered as she glanced around her friends. The last thing she needed was for one of them to notice the blush on her cheeks. 'Unless he can make a coffee as well as he can mark a footy, I won't need him.' She kept her tone light and hoped no-one heard the quake in her voice. 'How did you hear about that?'

Zara laughed. 'Are you kidding? How long have you lived in Glengarrick? Anything that happens in the main street is public knowledge. There are no secrets in this place. I reckon five minutes after Jed walked into the café, I heard about it up at the pub. I also heard you guys rescued a koala this morning. Not just one local hero, but two of you.'

Georgie rolled her eyes. 'Hardly.'

'Who wants a beer?' Jack asked, opening the lid of an esky. Georgie could have hugged him for changing the subject.

'How good is it to be back?' Ben asked.

'I *love* being back—' Emma said.

'As long as it's not longer than a weekend,' Kate finished for her.

They laughed.

'Does anyone know if Mr. All-Australian AFL star is still coming?' Jack asked. There was no malice in his voice—just admiration.

When no-one answered Jack's question, Georgie looked up. She was met with a circle of smiling faces. 'Why are you all looking at me?'

'We figured after your little rendezvous with Jed in the café yesterday and again today, he might have mentioned his plans,' Jack said with a smirk.

Georgie playfully elbowed him. 'He said he's coming.'

Ben looked up at the sky. 'He'll want to get here soon or the whole night will be washed out.'

The conversation circled back around to the weather and what everyone was up to. There was still no sign of Jed.

'Who's hungry?' Without waiting for an answer Zara pulled food from her esky and soon the table was covered with aluminium containers of food. Georgie had offered to bring food from the café but Zara had said it was her turn to do the catering. Instead, it looked like she'd conned the chef at the pub to prepare food for them.

As Georgie was ungracefully sucking the meat off a sticky honey and soy-coated chicken wing, she looked up and her eyes met Jed's. Her stomach twisted in pleasure.

As always, he looked great. It didn't seem to matter what clothes he wore, Jed could never blend into a crowd. Tonight he was dressed the same as most of the other guys—boots, jeans and a puffer jacket, but with his height and build he always stood out. It might have had something to do with his eyes and smile too.

Jack whistled and waved him over.

Jed smiled and waved back, but before he could get to their table, a dozen or so kids of all ages, decked out in the blue and white colours of the Cats, rushed him. It was as if they'd been anticipating his arrival more than Georgie had, and spent the last half hour looking at the gate every few minutes.

'Do you think he needs our help?' Charlie asked with a chuckle.

It wasn't only kids milling around now, but adults had flocked towards him. Many of them would have known him from when he grew up in Glengarrick, but others had clearly heard he was in town for the Grand Final and they wanted a chance to meet him.

Georgie watched them milling around, imagining them extending their congratulations on his career, offering their apologies it had ended because of injury, and asking him what he planned to do now. He offered everyone friendly smiles, answered questions and signed footballs, the back of jerseys and scraps of paper. Not once did he seem to be bothered by the attention or act like he wished he were anywhere else. Georgie's already high estimation of him skyrocketed.

By the time the crowd around Jed had thinned, Georgie had finished eating. She licked the remaining sauce off her fingers, cleaned them with a wipe, and stood. '*Now* I think he needs help.'

She wandered over near to where he stood with a young boy and her mum.

'Alright, buddy,' she heard him say, 'this is the last one, okay? I need to go and catch up with my friends over there before they eat all the food and don't leave me any.'

He signed his name, posed for one last picture, then smiled at Georgie. He started to walk towards her when a boy in a wheelchair was pushed in front of him.

'Excuse me, would you mind signing this please?' The boy, who looked to be around ten, held up a brand new, shiny red football.

Jed smiled at the boy and squatted in front of his chair. 'Sure can, my man. What's your name?'

'Theodore. Mum and Dad call me Teddy.' He leaned closer and brought one hand to the side of his face and cupped his mouth. 'But you can call me Franklin.'

Jed lifted his head. 'Really? Why is that?'

'Well, the twenty-sixth president of the United States was called Theodore. That's who I'm named after. But his fifth cousin, Franklin Delano Roosevelt, was the thirty-second president of the United States and he was in a wheelchair too. That's why my friends call me Franklin. Or FDR.'

Jed chuckled. 'You sure know your American history.' He leaned closer and whispered, 'am I allowed to call you Franklin or is that just for your friends?'

Teddy beamed. 'You can call me Franklin.'

Jed glanced up at his parents and smiled. 'G'day. Nice to meet you.' He took the ball from Teddy and tossed it in the air. 'I'm happy to sign it, mate, but not until we've played a bit of kick to kick. What do you reckon?'

Teddy's eyes widened into dinner plates and he fidgeted in his wheelchair, bobbing his head wildly.

Jed stood. 'Is that okay with you?' he asked Teddy's parents.

Beaming, they nodded.

'He's been nagging us to let him play football since last year,' Teddy's mum said. 'He's obsessed with AFL and the Cats and lately he's become obsessed with you. We had no idea you were here until we overheard someone talking about you. We didn't mean to interrupt.' She glanced at Georgie. 'I don't want to take you away from your friends.'

Georgie smiled at Teddy's mum. 'You're not interrupting anything.'

Georgie followed Jed as he pushed Teddy in his wheelchair to an open space away from the tables and chairs dotted around the picnic area. As if realising what was about to happen, people abandoned their baskets and eskies and followed Jed like he was playing a magical, musical pipe.

After Jed wheeled Teddy to one end of the grassy area, he took ten long steps away from him. 'How's your marking skills?' he called out.

Teddy opened his arms wide. 'How good are you off the left boot?' he cheekily replied.

Everyone laughed. Jed was a leftie.

'He's not very co-ordinated,' Teddy's dad said. 'Go easy.'

'He'll be fine,' Jed assured him.

For the next ten minutes, Jed patiently alternated between handballing and kicking the ball straight into Teddy's lap. Once Teddy caught the ball, Jed jogged back to him, scooped it up and repeated the move.

Everyone whistled and cheered them on as Teddy's parents videoed the whole thing. Soon some of Teddy's friends joined in and suddenly twenty kids were playing footy, taking it in turns to spin Teddy in his wheelchair or help him to pass the ball. No-one cared that it was cold, and the wind was whipping the clouds into a frenzy, threatening rain. After watching the joy in Teddy's face, the fireworks would be an anticlimax.

Georgie couldn't take her eyes off Jed. He was a natural with kids. He might have no idea what he was supposed to do next, but Georgie had an inkling it needed to involve working with children.

After signing Teddy's football, Jed posed for a few more photos, shook Teddy's parents by the hand then walked with Georgie back to the picnic table where the others waited. The turn in the weather had put a lot of people off and the crowd quickly dispersed as those with young families headed home. The others headed off too, which left only Zara, Georgie and Jed around the table.

Thunder rumbled in the distance. Jed glanced up at the overcast sky. 'Looks like I've missed my chance for some food.'

'No chance,' Georgie said with a laugh. 'You should see how much food Zara still has in her esky.' She didn't want this moment with Jed to end and if she had to hold an umbrella over his head while he ate, she would.

'And Jack left a case of beer,' Zara said. 'Want one?'

Jed nodded. 'That'd be great, thanks.'

Georgie waited for Jed to sit before she handed him a chicken Caesar salad wrap. 'Sorry, you've missed the chicken wings, but these are great.'

'So are the sausage rolls,' Zara said. 'Although they're

probably cold by now.' She removed the lid on the plastic container and pushed them towards him along with a bottle of tomato sauce.

'Cold food doesn't bother me.' Jed popped a sausage roll in his mouth.

'You were so good with Teddy,' Georgie said.

A flush crept up Jed's neck as if the compliment embarrassed him. He finished chewing and swallowed. 'Just doing what anyone else would do. He's a cool kid.'

'I'll bet you made his year,' Georgie replied. 'He'll probably remember this day for the rest of his life.'

'All it takes is one person. If I didn't have people around me when I was younger, who knows where I would have ended up. I still remember being around his age when I started playing Auskick. Some of the coaches I had were more like a dad to me than my own father was.'

There was a long beat of silence. They all knew about Jed's father.

'Have you ever considered being that "one person" for someone else? Someone like Teddy?' Georgie asked. 'They're always looking for help on the high school football team. Or maybe you could go back to uni and become a teacher.'

Jed glanced up at her with an odd look on his face. 'I'd never thought about doing that.'

'I think you'd make an exceptional teacher,' Georgie said.

Zara put her elbows on the picnic table and leaned in. 'Can I ask you something, Jed?'

Jed finished chewing and swallowed. 'Sure.' He took a swig of his beer.

'What's next?' she asked.

Jed looked from Georgie to Zara. 'Ah, the million-dollar question. I was talking to Georgie about this earlier today. My agent is currently looking into some possible jobs for me.'

'Coaching?' Zara asked, with a surprised look on her face.

'Assistant coaching. Maybe. I'm not sure. I love footy, but I love *playing* footy. I don't know if I could handle coaching from the sidelines and watching the guys get to play every week.'

'What about the farm? Would you consider coming back here to help your mum run it?' Zara asked.

He stared straight ahead as he took another mouthful of beer. 'Another million-dollar question. The short answer: I don't know. I broached it with Mum, but she's worried about me getting stuck here.'

Georgie sensed there was more to it than that. Everyone in town knew that after Jed's father gambled away the family's entire life savings, Michelle clung onto as much of the farm as she could. If she was too proud or embarrassed to accept Jed's help— financial or otherwise—it was hardly surprising after everything she'd gone through.

'Do *you* think you'd get tied down if you stayed?' Georgie

asked.

He shrugged. 'Like I said to you earlier, I just don't know.'

'One more question,' Zara said.

Jed chuckled. 'Any more and I'll start charging you. In case you haven't heard, I'm unemployed now. I could use the extra money.'

'Is there anything keeping you in Geelong, or Melbourne, now you're not playing football?'

'Not really. I have a house in Geelong, but I could easily sell it or put tenants in it.'

'Is there a WAG in your life? No wife or girlfriend waiting for you in the wings?' Zara asked. 'Or in the forward pocket or whatever you call it?'

'What's with the third degree, Zazu? Are you asking for yourself, or a friend?'

Zara nudged him with her elbow. 'Mate, if push came to shove, I'd turn for you, but I don't think my girlfriend would be too happy about that.'

Jed laughed. 'There's no WAG. Happy?'

Georgie stayed silent and chewed on a nail and let Zara ask all the questions she wanted answers to. He hadn't mentioned anyone, but that didn't mean he didn't have a girlfriend he was keeping quiet. No significant other was good news for Georgie.

'Do you date much?' Zara asked.

Jed balled up the paper wrapping from the chicken wrap and

basketball tossed it in the nearby rubbish bin before grabbing a bag of corn chips. Opening the packet, he popped a few chips into his mouth and crunched on them before replying.

'I date now and then.'

'You're good at evading questions.'

He smiled. 'Being asked questions is an occupational hazard and yeah, I'm an expert. Like you're an expert at asking them. Typical lawyer. What do you want to know, Zazu? Do you want a list of the women I've seen in the last six months and their phone numbers?'

'Do you have a list?'

He threw back his head and laughed. 'For a moment I thought you were serious.'

'I am,' she deadpanned.

'There's no-one special.' He flicked a look in Georgie's direction then eyeballed Zara again. 'You can tell your friend.'

Zara grinned. 'Oh, trust me. I will.'

'My turn for a question,' he said.

Zara shrugged. 'Sure.'

'Not you. This one's for Georgie.'

Georgie froze. He wasn't going to ask about her dating history, was he? She couldn't admit she'd never had a relationship that lasted longer than a few dates except for Neil. And Neil's name was in the never-to-be-mentioned category. Everyone knew that. For some reason, the idea of Jed knowing what happened between her and Neil was embarrassing.

'What's next for *you,* Georgie? What big dreams are you chasing?'

With his focus fixed firmly on her, Georgie blinked and forced herself to swallow. She needed a few extra seconds to allow her to concoct something that sounded exciting. The truth was, she'd never breathed a word to anyone about her dream. Saying it aloud might sound crazy. It was better to let him think she was already living her dream.

'Well…' she began. 'As you know, I have the café now, and I'm running that largely on my own, and so—'

Jed's raised eyebrows stopped her. 'That's not what I asked. I know the café isn't your dream.'

She licked her lips. How did he know that? She glanced at Zara, but her friend suddenly found something interesting to look at on her phone.

'What do you *want* to do?' Jed asked softly.

She stared at him. No one—not her parents, not her teachers, not even Zara—had asked her that question. She cleared her throat.

'I want to bring hope,' she said, as equally softly.

Zara looked up and a flicker of interest crossed Jed's face, but they both stayed quiet and didn't prod or push her. Then and there Georgie decided she liked Jed even more. She trusted him.

'I used to always want to be a nurse. And maybe that's something I'd still like to do, but what I'd really love is to run camps for kids. I want to have week-long camps for kids who need respite from their parents.' The words tumbled out and she rushed on before she lost confidence. 'There are already plenty of programs for kids with mental health challenges, but I want to run something for the kids who are struggling with *parents* who have mental health illnesses. It's tough on them.'

As an adult she struggled living with a parent with a mental illness so she could imagine how hard it was for kids and teenagers.

'Why have you never mentioned that to me?' Zara asked.

'I know it probably sounds silly but—'

Jed cut her off. 'It doesn't sound silly at all. It sounds incredible.'

The wind whipped up and the empty beer cans the others had left on the table scattered like skittles. As Zara stood and started picking things up and putting them in the rubbish bin, large drops of rain fell.

'I guess that means they'll cancel the fireworks,' Georgie said.

She tried to stand, but the ground was slippery and suddenly she was on her back staring at the darkening sky with a searing pain on the right side of her head where she must have whacked it against the table on her way down. What a klutz. She closed her eyes and willed the pain away.

'Let's get you up.'

Before she could protest, Jed's hands were under her arms. He scooped her up and placed her gently on the seat, kneeling in front of her. The drops of rain had turned into a steady drizzle and his hair was wet, plastering it across his forehead. Forgetting the pain in her head, she wanted to wipe his hair away from his face so she could see his eyes. She took a deep breath to steady her racing pulse and stop the butterflies from taking flight in her stomach but failed on both counts.

Zara shoved Jed aside and squatted in front of her. Her eyebrows knit together. 'Are you okay?'

No. Definitely not okay. But that was because she wanted to kiss Jed. 'I'm fine. The only thing hurt is my pride.'

'Do I need to get the St Johns First Aid people?'

Georgie shook her head, frowning with the hum of pain. She screwed her eyes shut in a grimace. 'I think I'm okay. Give me a minute.'

'Let's survey the damage.'

Georgie opened her eyes slowly and stared straight into Jed's again. He'd edged Zara out of the way.

'I don't think it's too bad,' he said, touching the side of her head.

A shiver went through her.

Déjà vu.

'Bit of a bump, but no blood.' His voice was husky, and his eyes were filled with unspoken worry.

Or was it something else?

'I'll drive you home,' he offered.

She attempted to pull off a smile. 'I can drive. My car is here.'

'You're not driving home after a knock to the head.'

Zara grabbed an esky in each hand. 'I've got no idea where Jack's gone, but he'll have to come back and pick up his own esky. It's still full of drinks.'

'I'll take it,' Jed said, grabbing the handle from her. 'I can drop it off to his place tomorrow.'

The rain was heavier now, and they were getting soaked.

'Okay, Jed. She's all yours. Get her home safe, won't you?' After giving Georgie a quick hug, Zara dashed off towards the car park.

'Do you think you can walk?' Jed asked.

'I'm not going to let you carry me, if that's what you're asking,' she replied, trying to laugh. 'I feel okay,' she lied. She touched the burgeoning bump on her head. 'Although I probably need to ice this.'

'Come on.'

They hurried towards the exit. Hers and Jed's were the only cars left in the car park.

'I can drive.'

'No. You can get your car tomorrow.'

Halfway across the parking lot, the rain came down in earnest, pelting their faces and moulding their clothes to their bodies. By the time Jed unlocked the passenger side of his SUV and opened the door for her, Georgie was drenched. And cold.

He shoved the esky on the back seat then went around the front of the car and slid behind the wheel, slamming the door. A flash of lightning lit the sky, followed moments later by thunder.

'Wow.'

'That was close.'

She burst out laughing and Jed joined her. Wiping away laughter-tears from her eyes she pushed her wet hair behind her ears then shivered. Jed turned in his seat and fished on the floor in the back for something. He pulled out a navy-blue Cats training jacket and handed it to her then pulled out a towel.

'Take off your wet coat and put this on.' He jabbed a button on the dash and the car started. 'I'll turn on the heater and seat warmers too.'

'You're wetter than I am,' she said. At least she had her puffer jacket. It was soaked, but underneath she was relatively dry, just cold.

'I'm fine. Have you ever watched a game of footy? I'm used to a bit of bad weather.'

'True.'

She recalled one of the last matches she'd watched him play in conditions worse than this. The players had skidded their way over the wet ground as if they were on a giant Slip 'N Slide.

In one fluid move, Jed removed his wet jumper, revealing a long sleeve T-shirt that hugged his well-defined muscles. An instant picture formed in her mind of him in the gym, lifting weights, muscles pumping, sweat glistening on bronzed skin. He took the T-shirt off and her gaze dropped lower to his abs. Her heart rate accelerated, and she quickly forced her eyes back to his face. She wasn't cold anymore.

Beads of water dripped off his hair and taking the towel from his hands, Georgie leaned towards him and carefully dried his hair and face. When she slipped her hands down his neck to his chest, he grabbed her wrists.

They were both breathing heavily, and the windscreen was completely fogged over.

'Georgie.'

If it was a warning, she disregarded it. Feeling reckless, she slowly ran the towel across Jed's shoulders, over his pecs and down the centre of his chest towards his jeans. When she reached the buckle of his belt, he sucked in a deep breath and closed his eyes.

'Georgie.'

It *was* a warning. One she couldn't ignore.

She pulled her hands away and folded them in her lap, feigning innocence. 'I don't want you to catch a cold.'

'Trust me, Georgie, I'm that hot right now, it'll never happen.'

She stared at him.

'Each time I'm near you I want to touch you again.' He swore softly and put his hands on the steering wheel, clenching and unclenching them. 'I need to you get home.'

He put the car in reverse and backed out.

Chapter 11

As Georgie tugged his jacket tighter around her shoulders, rested her head back against the seat, and closed her eyes, Jed tried not to overthink what had just happened. The feel of her warm hands on his bare skin had done all sorts of unexpected damage to his self-control. He needed to get her home before he pulled over and kissed her senseless.

The further they got out of town, the worse the storm was, bringing back memories of the night he'd come across her car down the gully. He drove slowly and carefully, struggling to see through the windshield at times. Eventually, he turned onto her road, then braked suddenly.

Georgie's eyes snapped open and she sat up, bracing herself with her palms on the dashboard. 'What's wrong?'

'There's a tree across the road. I won't be able to get through.' He made a split-second decision. 'I'll take you back to my place.' He glanced over at her. 'If that's okay?'

She shivered. 'Of course.'

When they arrived at the farm, they bolted the fifty metres from the shed where he parked his car to the house. At the back door, Georgie shook off his jacket and toed off her shoes.

'I think you should take a shower.'

Her eyes grew wide and dark. For a split second he had thoughts of scooping her up and carrying her to the bathroom. His skin, which had been on a slow simmer in the car was now a blistering boil. He took a step back, then another, trying to ignore the throb in his groin.

'I'll let Mum know you're here.' He motioned to a door and tried not to look at her or think of her standing in his shower with water cascading over her body. 'The bathroom's in there. Put your clothes outside the door and I'll toss them in the dryer while you take a shower. I'll find something you can throw on.' She was as stiff as a board. Whether from nerves or because she was cold or both, he wasn't sure. He touched her arm and smiled to put her at ease. 'Take your time okay? There's plenty of hot water.'

She nodded and closed the door behind her. Moments later the door opened, and she dropped her soggy clothes on the floor. He scooped them up and took them to the laundry.

He was loading the dryer when his mother walked in.

'I thought I heard a car.' She frowned. 'Who's in your bathroom?'

'Georgina Purcell.'

The frown turned into a smile.

He'd never bought a girlfriend home so he hastily explained before Mum got the wrong idea. 'We got caught in the storm down at the river. They had to cancel the fireworks. I was driving Georgie home, but a tree has come down across the road near her place and we couldn't get through.'

Mum's smile fell, replaced by concern. 'Did you call the SES? They'll want to know.'

'No.'

'I'll give Mal a call and tell him.' She touched his arm. 'Look after her.'

'Of course.'

In his bedroom he opened one of his duffle bags full of merchandise he'd collected over the years. Rifling through it, he pulled out a pair of Cats branded women's pyjamas he'd planned to give Mum. They'd fit Georgie perfectly. He also had a men's velour dressing gown he couldn't imagine ever wearing, but it would keep Georgie warm while her clothes dried.

Mum knocked before sticking her head around his open bedroom door. 'Is Georgie staying the night?'

'Um…I…ah…'

Without waiting for his reply, she bustled out, muttering something about the bed in the spare room not having clean sheets on it.

He glanced at his king-size bed, only one side slept in. More than enough room for him and Georgie. And the sheets were clean.

A picture of the two of them intertwined under the covers flashed before him and he quickly clamped his eyes shut. No. He couldn't go there. Could he? But if she *did* stay the night in the spare room next to his, how was he supposed to sleep?

While Georgie showered, he changed into a pair of trackpants and a hoodie. He would have a shower later. A cold one if necessary.

Leaving the pyjamas and dressing gown at the bathroom door for Georgie, he headed to the kitchen to see if there was anything to eat.

Ten minutes later Georgie appeared. He let his eyes rake slowly from her hair to her bare toes. She'd clearly found the hair dryer under the sink and her hair was a halo of brown around her shoulders. The dressing gown tie was wrapped twice around her waist and it fell to her feet where he caught a glimpse of hot pink nail polish.

'Do you need socks?' His mouth was dry. Turning, he gestured to the kitchen table. 'Take a seat.'

He strode down the hall to his bedroom and found a pair of thick socks. Returning to the kitchen he tossed them to her. He couldn't afford to get to close. Even from a distance, she smelled of a mixture of citrus and vanilla. All he could think about was pulling her into a hug and crushing her to his chest.

And kissing her.

Her eyes darkened and seemed to burn into his. Had he spoken out loud or did she feel it too?

After putting on the socks she stood and took a step towards him. 'Does your mum know I'm here?' Her voice was low and husky.

He nodded. His mouth was dry and he wasn't sure he'd be able to speak. 'I think she's making up the bed in the spare room. And she was going to call Mal someone about the tree on the road.'

'Malcolm Kennedy. He's in charge of the SES.'

'Right. What about your mum? Will she be worried about you?'

'She probably won't know I'm gone.' Her shoulders dropped. 'I'll call her though.'

'She'll want to know you're safe.' He took a step towards her, then another. Grasping the collar of the thick gown, he gently pulled her closer. 'Georgie Purcell, do you have any idea what you're doing to me?' His voice was raspy. He smoothed the lapels on the gown, feeling the curve of her breasts beneath it and under that, her pounding heart. 'Sorry it's a little large.'

'At least it's warm,' she replied, not taking her eyes off him.

He slipped his hand behind her neck and ran his fingers through her hair, brushing it away from the nape of her neck. He'd been trying not to touch her from the moment he'd walked into her café, but he'd used up every last ounce of restraint. Her eyes were wide, her mouth slightly open. He had no idea where his mother was, but he prayed she didn't walk in on them right now, because he needed to do something about those parted lips.

'Jed…'

'Georgie…'

They both spoke at the same time.

'When you look at me like that…' he began.

She tilted her head back and he bent to meet her halfway. The touch of her lips on his broke any semblance of control. He slipped his arms from her face to her back and pulled her closer. At first her kiss was tentative, and for a split second he considered stopping. Then she sighed and relaxed in his arms and he swept restraint to a back corner of his mind.

When she raised her arms and threaded her fingers through his hair, he kissed her harder. She opened her mouth and his tongue slid over hers, before dancing around it. He'd intended to kiss her once, lightly, and let her go, but the more she responded to his kisses, the more his passion flared and blazed into a ferocious need. There was no stopping now.

He lowered his hands and slipped them inside the gown reaching for her waist. Even with the barrier of his clothes and the flannel pyjamas she wore, his body surged with red hot desire for her. The world tilted and his mind went into free fall. He was caught between wanting her right now and knowing they shouldn't be crossing this threshold again. If he kept holding her, he'd want to hold her forever and he had no idea if that's what she wanted too.

He pulled back and ended the kiss, lowering his arms to his sides.

Confusion crossed her face followed by disappointment.

'Not here.' He ran his hands over his face, regretting his sharp tone. 'Not now,' he said, more gently. 'Not with Mum around somewhere.'

She nodded.

Jed took a step back, needing to put physical distance between them. There was nothing he could do about the emotional distance between them though.

He shouldn't have kissed her again.

All it took was one kiss and he was transported straight back to that night he'd first held her in his arms and comforted her after the storm. Ever since then, no other woman he'd met had caused him to feel the way he'd felt around Georgie.

Life would be much better with her in it, but he wasn't sure if he was in a place where he was ready to invite a woman into his life. There was so much uncertainty in his future. He had no job, no career pathway, no plan. He didn't even know where he wanted to live. Right now, he had nothing to offer Georgie. And what if he decided to stay and she decided she wanted to leave? She'd told him of dream of a camp for kids, but she'd never said anything about wanting it to be located in Glengarrick.

He let out a soft sigh. Based on the way she'd kissed him

back, he suspected their experience in bed as adults would be earthshattering, but nothing would be solved by sleeping with her tonight. He had to find safer ground to stop himself from thinking of her lying beside him in bed.

'Are you hungry?' he asked. Food fixed everything and getting her something to eat would put space between them.

'Not really. But I'd love a cup of tea.'

'Kettle's already boiled.'

His mum appeared in the doorway. 'Hello, Georgina. Good to see you.'

'Hello Mrs. Delaney.'

'Sweetheart, I think you're old enough to call me Michelle.'

Georgie smiled. 'Thanks for letting me stay the night. Jed said you wouldn't mind.'

'Not at all. It's a wild night out there. I've just gotten off the phone to Mal. They've had a dozen calls already from people who have lost rooves and there are trees down over roads everywhere. I'm going down to the headquarters to see if I can help. Behave yourselves and don't wait up for me.' With a wave, Michelle opened the back door and swept out into the dark night.

Jed laughed. 'Behave ourselves,' he repeated. 'What does she think we are? Teenagers?' He turned to Georgie, surprised to see how pale she was. 'Are you okay?'

She chewed her bottom lip. 'Maybe I should try to get home.' She looked up at him. 'Or maybe I should open up the café in case people need something to eat.'

'Call your mother first,' he said. 'She's probably fine. Then we can decide what to do.'

Georgie's hands shook as she picked up her phone to all her mother. She put the phone to her ear and turned her back to him. It seemed to take forever before the call was answered.

'Hey, Mum.' Georgie raised her voice half an octave and it was clear she was trying to inject a positive tone in her voice. 'You okay? It's a pretty bad storm out there…I'm fine….yes, they cancelled the fireworks…I'm going to stay at Jed Delaney's…There's a tree over the road and I couldn't get through…I can come home if you need me…' Her shoulders sagged. 'Okay. I'll see you tomorrow. Will you come to the game?' Silence. 'Okay. No worries.'

She disconnected the call and dropped the phone on the kitchen table. Her eyes were moist.

'You okay?' he asked carefully.

'Fine.'

He pulled her into a hug and rested his chin on her head. 'You must miss your dad when …' His voice trailed off. 'Sorry. I've probably put my foot in my mouth.'

'It's okay.' She gave him a smile. 'I mean, yeah, I do miss him, a lot, especially when Mum's like this. But life goes on. It has to.'

'But not for your mum.'

She shook her head. 'No. It's been seven years since he passed and each anniversary I hope she'll somehow miraculously snap out of it.'

'Seven years. Wow. Feels like yesterday we were all hanging around together at school.'

She nodded. 'Yep. Ten years. Blink and you miss it.'

Neither of them said anything for a while. He wondered if she was remembering the night they'd slept together.

'Why do I worry more about my mother than she does?' Her voice was a whisper. 'And why do I put her happiness ahead of my own and wish I didn't have to? What kind of daughter does that make me, Jed?'

He didn't hesitate. 'An honest one.' He pressed a tender kiss to her temple.

More silence settled between them.

'How's that bump?' he asked after a while.

She massaged her head. 'To be honest, I'd forgotten about it.'

'No headache?'

'A little.'

'You're not dizzy?'

'No. Honestly, I'm fine.'

And that was Georgie's problem. Zara was right. Georgie was "fine", but she wasn't happy. He could see it in her eyes. She was existing. He turned her hand over and tenderly stroked her palm. 'Whenever you want to talk, I'm here. I'll listen.'

She gave him an attempt at a brave smile. 'Thank you, Jed. That means a lot.' She stood on tiptoes and kissed his cheek. 'I might hit the sack.' She hesitated before grinning. 'And don't worry. I heard your mum. We have to "behave".' She used her fingers to make air quotes.

He grinned back as memories of the past flared again. 'When have I ever behaved? And when have I ever done what Mum told me to do?'

Without thought, he pulled Georgie into his arms and kissed her. Then, without another word, he led her to his bedroom. And she followed.

Exactly like last time.

Chapter 12

Ten Years Earlier

Jed forced his eyes open. He wasn't in his bed. He sat up, but a wave of dizziness knocked him back again. His brain felt like it was going through some sort of weird reboot. A numbing sensation rushed through him and he closed his eyes again and fought against the taste of bile in the back of his throat. A low buzz sounded followed by a ringing in his ears. Slowly his hearing returned, and the sound of rushing water registered.

Where was he?

He tried to open his eyes again and when he did, he saw nothing above him except a foggy inky blackness.

Someone was talking, but he felt like he was under water and he couldn't make out what they were saying. Everything was moving in slow motion.

Piece by piece, like the gradual lifting of a fog that had descended over his senses, he put together what had happened.

Out of nowhere a tree branch had hit him. Hard.

He remembered Georgie diving one way as he'd gone the other.

Heart hammering, he sat up. Where was she? Was she okay?

'Georgie.' He bellowed. 'Georgie!'

'Jed!'

Thank God. Relief washed over him, and he fell back against the wet ground and slipped back into darkness.

When he woke again, he had no idea how long he'd been out to it. The first thing he saw when his vision cleared was Georgie's face. Tears streamed down her cheeks. Or it might have been rain. He blinked, trying to shift the spots in front of him. The edges of his vision flickered and danced but refused to come into focus. It felt like a thunderstorm had exploded inside his head.

After a while the disjointed haze receded enough for him to start making sense of his surroundings. The initial whirlwind of confusion subsided, and memories filtered back sluggishly. It was like watching a movie in slow motion or a video that kept buffering.

'Jed. Jed. Can you hear me?'

He pushed himself up, but his sight blurred again. He tried to fight his eyes to keep them from closing, but it was like they had a mind of their own.

Warm hands cupped his face. 'Open your eyes, Jed.'

He obeyed because she sounded so insistent.

'Do you think you can walk?'

He nodded, then grimaced as the pain spun the insides of his head. Rolling onto his hands and knees he pushed himself upright and fought against a wave of nausea. Holding onto Georgie's arm for support, he staggered and stumbled up the steep muddy embankment to the road. The rain had eased but the wind was bitterly cold, and it was whipping droplets of water off the trees, soaking him through his clothes down to his skin. He looked at Georgie. She was saturated too.

'I need to get you to hospital,' she said, teeth chattering.

His brain was struggling to work in a linear fashion. He had a vague memory they'd already had this discussion, but if he'd been knocked out, he couldn't go to hospital. They'd ask too many questions.

'No.'

She blinked. 'But you're hurt.'

'So are you.' He touched her blood-streaked face, recalling she had a gash to her head. What if it needed stitches?

They stood on the side of the road in the pouring rain and stared at each other. They were in a hot mess.

'If we go to the hospital, they'll want to know what happened.' He waited for her to connect the dots but perhaps she wouldn't. 'I'm supposed to be playing footy this weekend. If the coach finds out I got knocked out, I won't be allowed to play. It's the prelim.'

He had recruiters coming to watch him play and if he played

well, there was every chance he'd get drafted. He couldn't stuff up that opportunity. It might be the only chance he got to leave Glengarrick.

The blood drained from Georgie's face and fresh tears formed in her eyes. 'What am I going to do? How will I explain what happened to Zara's car?'

'We'll figure something out. But first, let's go back to my place so we can get cleaned up.'

'But what will we tell your parents—'

'They're away for the weekend. I can take you back to our house and at least get you cleaned up.' Had he just said that? His mind was playing tricks on him.

Georgie was breathing too quickly, as if she was about to hyperventilate. He pulled her into his arms. 'We'll figure something out,' he repeated. 'Maybe we can make it look like you slipped and hit your head or something.' Even to him, the excuse didn't sound plausible. And it didn't explain why Georgie was driving Zara's car and how it had ended up in the creek.

'I need to call Zara.'

'You need to call your parents first.'

She nodded, clearly conflicted. 'I'll tell Mum I'm staying at Zara's.'

He frowned. 'Where *will* you stay?'

She briefly snagged her bottom lip with her teeth and looked up at him. 'If your parents are away, would it be okay if I stayed at yours?'

'I guess so.'

'Thank you.'

With shaking hands, she called her mum.

'Hi, Mum…Yes, I'm okay…Everything's fine. I'm going to stay at Zara's, okay? Uh-huh…I'll see you tomorrow…my battery's about to die.'

She put the phone back in her pocket and exhaled slowly. 'Mum bought my story'

'She won't check?'

She shook her head. 'No. I stay there all the time.'

'What about Zara's parents? What if they talk to your mum?'

She crossed her fingers. 'I have to hope they don't.'

'What are we going to tell them about the car?'

'Maybe Zara can tell her parents we were driving through the creek and we didn't realise how high the water was. We could say we got a puncture and when we got out to check it, the water pushed the car down the creek. That way it wouldn't *all* be a lie. And I'd be omitting the fact I was actually driving the car.'

He digested Georgie's story. 'It *could* work.' Opening the passenger door of his car he climbed in.

Georgie peered into the car then at him. 'What are you doing?'

'You'll have to drive. Sorry, Georgie. My head is spinning.' It was more than spinning. It was oscillating like a fan on high speed.

'But I don't have my license.'

'Another reason why we need to come up with a good story. Where did you say Zara is?'

'It's a long story.'

She turned the key in the ignition and clutched the steering wheel with white knuckles. Was she going to be okay to drive?

'I'll be okay,' she said, reading his mind.

When they arrived at his place, Georgie helped him out of the car. The moment his feet hit the ground, he realised how much his head hurt. Worse than any knock he'd ever had in footy. He'd never experienced concussion, and if that's what this was, he never wanted to be knocked out again.

He glanced at Georgie. She looked dreadful. She was pale and the blood had dried down both sides of her head and clotted in her hair. He needed to get her inside and clean her up. Taking her hand, he led her inside, past the kitchen and down the hallway to his bedroom. While she perched on the end of his bed, he went into the bathroom, returning a moment later with a first aid kit.

'We've had this for years, so God only knows what's in it.' He brushed a piece of Georgie's matted hair away from her forehead. He wanted to see how deep the wound was. Hopefully it was only superficial and wouldn't need stitching. 'Sorry. This is going to sting.' He dipped a cotton wool ball soaked in antiseptic and touched it to her skin.

By the time he'd cleaned away the dried blood and inspected the wound, he was fairly certain she wouldn't need stitches. She might end up with a scar, but it would be hidden by her hair. As he applied steri-strips and a dressing, he'd never felt so relieved in his life.

As he was putting things back in the first aid kit, Georgie's phone rang.

The colour drained from her cheeks. 'It's Zara,' she whispered. 'What will I tell her?'

'The truth.'

Through sobs, Georgie explained what had happened and outlined her plan for how they would cover for each other. Jed sat quietly, listening to her, grateful she didn't mention anything to Zara about him being knocked out by the tree.

After she hung up, she turned to him and exhaled slowly. 'Zara won't say a word.'

'What about her car?'

'It's insured. She said her parents will buy the story. They'll just be relieved we're okay.'

He released his breath slowly too. He hated lying, but if his coach found out he'd been concussed, he wouldn't be allowed to play for two weeks meaning he'd miss the next two games. And potentially miss the chance to prove himself to the recruiters. No way that was going to happen. After some sleep, he'd be fine.

'Thanks for not telling Zara I got hit on the head.'

'I had to tell her you'd rescued me though.'

Suddenly tears streamed down her cheeks and she brought her

hands up to hide her face. Jed's heart ached for her as he pulled her into his arms. He let her cry against his chest for a few minutes before she collected herself and pulled back. He gently wiped the tears from her cheeks while she dabbed at his shirt and apologised for making a mess of it. His heart pounded so loudly he was surprised she couldn't hear it.

'Sorry, Jed. I guess it's just hit me how bad tonight could have been.'

'The main thing is, we're both okay.'

As if his body was moving on its own accord, he reached for her again and took her in his arms. The instinct that surged through him was so strong it evaded the "what-am-I-doing" thoughts he should have been having. Taking another step closer he cupped her face in his hands and kissed her.

Her lips were soft, and the kiss was so sweet it was like a hit of sugar into his body. He revelled in the taste of her mouth, the touch of her skin against his fingertips, and the way her body pressed close to his. She let out a breathy sound against his mouth and kissed him back, and every synapse in his body screamed into life. She was both heat and soft curves and he wanted her.

But like the screech of tyres on a wet road, his brain caught up with what they were doing. He stepped back and she looked up at him, dazed, with flushed cheeks and half-closed eyes.

'I'm sorry,' he said gruffly. 'Maybe we shouldn't—'

She drowned out his attempt at another apology with her lips.

At that, he forgot about the pain in his head. Forgot about the accident. Forgot everything except his desire for her. He ran his hands down her back to her bottom while their tongues duelled. He slowly took off her jumper and when their eyes met, all remaining strength, and any willpower he had, seeped away.

He took her hand and led her towards his bedroom, and she didn't hesitate. They'd come this far. They might as well go all the way.

At the doorway he paused. 'Are you sure this is what you want?'

She nodded, eyes shining. 'Yes, Jed, yes. I want this.'

'I want *you*,' he whispered.

She kissed him again and pleasure spiralled through him. Nothing other than that moment mattered. Not the storm, not the accident. Not even the future. All that mattered was they were here, now, together and he was never going to forget this night.

Chapter 13

A long, snake-like row of cars lined each side of the road leading to the football oval. Georgie had to double back to find a car park. Glengarrick had a population of less than nine hundred people and it always staggered her how many people came from out of town for the Grand Final every year.

She and Zara got out of Zara's car and walked up the middle of the road along with a steady flow of people ebbing around them. There were babies and toddlers in prams pushed by parents and grandparents. And she'd never seen so many dogs. Kids of all ages walked or rode bikes and scooters. Many of them were dressed in the red, white and black colours of the *Saints*.

The sun was slowly warming the air, but Georgie had layered up, knowing how cold it could get standing on the sidelines if the sun went behind the clouds and the wind picked up. The weather this time of year in the alpine region was so fickle. Yesterday she'd worn a pair of jeans and long-sleeved T-shirt, tomorrow she might need her thermals.

The twang of a banjo came through the speakers and pulsed through her body. Despite an aversion to country music, Georgie found herself walking in time to the beat. It suited the atmosphere and the scenery. As they waited at the gates, money in hand to pay the entrance fee, a voice over the sound system declared there were bargains to buy at the cake stall.

'We have to buy one of Mrs. Kennedy's prize-winning chocolate mud cakes,' Zara announced.

Georgie laughed. Zara said the same thing every year the second she stepped through the gates.

'Don't mock me. You know as well as I do, they're to die for,' Zara said with a pretend sniff. 'But we'll need to be quick. They always sell out first.'

The aroma from the Lion's Club tent, with its sausages and sizzling onions made Georgie's stomach growl. Then she spotted the mobile coffee van and the smell of freshly brewed coffee wafted towards her. Her mouth watered and she dragged Zara in that direction.

'Cake can wait. We need coffee.'

After coffee, she'd get a sausage and maybe a freshly-made hot jam donut—she'd spotted someone pouring batter into the hot oil a few tents away. Zara wasn't the only one who had her footy Grand Final traditions.

After grabbing their coffees, they headed in the direction of the ground. Every year, they got there early enough to pick a sunny spot on the wing. A little boy bumped into her; his eyes fixated on a balloon at the end of the string in his hand. His mother apologised to Georgie before they blended back into the sea of bodies. Georgie smiled at the woman, but she was already gone, chasing after her son.

'Georgie. Zara.'

They turned to see Jack and Emma coming their way.

'I thought Jed would be with you guys,' Jack said.

Georgie shook her head. 'He said he wanted to get to the ground early. I haven't seen him.' She *had* seen him—when he dropped her home earlier that morning, but no way was she admitting that to her friends. She was certain she'd fallen asleep wearing the afterglow-of-sex-smile and was scared to look in case it was permanently affixed to her face.

'Is he going to stand with us to watch?' Emma asked.

'I don't know.' He hadn't said much on the way to her house. Neither of them had. They'd held hands the whole way home and before she'd got out of the car, he'd given her a lingering kiss, but that was it. Talking was the last thing on their minds.

'We're going to sit closer to the goals,' Jack said. 'Where are you guys going?'

'The wing,' Zara replied.

'Catch you later.'

Emma and Jack said goodbye and the crowd soon swallowed

them up. A group of giggling girls dashed past, still dressed in their netball kits.

'Remember when we used to play?' Georgie asked as they skirted the netball courts. The earlier netball Grand Final had been played, but the court was still covered with parents and girls.

'I haven't picked up a netball since year twelve. Maybe I should investigate playing with a team in Melbourne,' Zara said. 'You should ask about joining a team here.'

'Not me. Knowing my luck, I'd do an ACL.'

They stopped walking and stood off to the side of a large purpose-built stage that would be used after the game for the presentation medals. On stage, a team of young Irish dancers stood, backs straight, arms bent as they waited for the music to begin. When the music started they stomped their little feet and flicked their legs in a complicated move. After watching a moment, Zara tugged Georgie's arm and they walked on a bit further.

They found the Uniting Church cake stall and surveyed the mouth-watering goods. Zara bought two of Mrs. Kennedy's famous chocolate mud cakes, but Georgie took her time deciding. She was deliberating between the lamingtons, the vanilla sponge cake, and the scones when she overheard something that made her heart gallop.

'Did you know Jed Delaney's thinking of moving back home,' a woman's voice cut across the sound of the crowd.

'Is he?' a second woman replied. 'And do what?'

Georgie tried to see who was speaking, but they were standing on the other side of the tent, out of view.

'There's nothing in Glengarrick for him.'

'What about the farm?' the first woman asked. 'His grandfather would have loved him to take it on.'

'I don't think Michelle Delaney will give it up that easily.'

The two women gossiped about Michelle for a while before their conversation circled back to Jed.

'What a shame he and Georgina Purcell didn't get together. Do you remember that song they sang for the *Glengarrick's Got Talent* thing?'

Georgie stiffened.

'Georgina's a sweet girl, but Jed's way out of her league. Anyway, I heard he has a girlfriend in Geelong.'

A weight dropped into Georgie's gut. Not about the less than favourable remark the woman had made about her. She looked at Zara who wore the same mask of confusion Georgie was sure was on her own face.

'Girlfriend?' Georgie mouthed.

Zara lifted her shoulders in a don't-ask-me expression.

Yesterday when Zara had asked him, Jed had emphatically stated he was single. No wife. No girlfriend. Had he lied? If so, why? A shiver ran up Georgie's spine and a cold sensation washed over her. If Jed had a girlfriend, why had he slept with her?

Suddenly she felt sick.

'Did you know Mrs. Kennedy uses a packet cake mix,' a voice beside them said.

They turned. It was Reece. Georgie strained to hear the rest of the women's conversation, but they had moved away out of earshot.

'Mrs. Kennedy wins first prize every year at the show and people pay her a truckload of money to make them cakes for special occasions. I can't believe she uses a bloody packet mix from Coles and claims she's made the cake from scratch.' Reece gave Georgie a conspiratorial wink. 'Reckon I should tell her?' he asked, pointing to a woman who was handing over a fifty-dollar note to buy two of the small chocolate mud cakes.

Zara groaned. 'Are you kidding me?' She held up the mud cakes she'd just purchased. 'I paid twenty dollars for these.'

'I would have made the same cake for ten.' Reece laughed. 'Anyway, good to see you girls. Enjoy the game and I'll see you at the pub tonight.' He waved and loped off.

'Georgina Purcell?'

Georgie turned to find a man blocking her path. She glanced down at his jeans and too clean RM Williams boots. Not a farmer. And not a local because she knew everyone in town.

He smiled, dimples deepening. 'It *is* Georgina Purcell, isn't it?'

'Georgie. Yes,' she replied cautiously.

'You're prettier than your Facebook profile photo.' He held his hand. 'Nick Pearce. Channel Seven.'

Georgie's mouth fell open. Forget the rude comment about her appearance, why had he been checking her Facebook account?

'I was talking to a friend of yours. She said you and Jed Delaney have a little thing going on.'

An uneasy feeling went through her. She glanced at Zara, who shrugged. Was this guy just looking for a story? If so, he'd come to the wrong people.

'Jed and I are friends,' Georgie said carefully, 'and before Friday I hadn't seen or spoken to him since he left Glengarrick. So, if you're trying to dig up dirt or something, you won't get any from me.'

Nick smiled. 'I'm not looking for dirt, trust me.'

'Good,' Zara said, folding her arms across her chest and standing tall. 'Because, like Georgie said, Jed doesn't have any.'

'Fair enough,' Nick said, taking a small step back. 'But I'd love to know what he was like when he was younger. You girls went to school with him. Did he ever do anything wrong? Step out of line? Tell a lie?' He chuckled. 'Seems like Jed's almost too perfect, which makes me wonder what secrets he's hiding.'

'Bark up another tree, Nick,' Zara said, glaring at him. 'Jed is our homegrown hero and you won't find a single person in this town who will say anything bad about him. Least of all us.'

Nick held up his hands. 'Sorry. I didn't mean to offend you.

I'm not looking for a bad news story, honest. I just wanted some background on him. I wondered if he had a girlfriend in town or something that had brought him back. The woman I spoke to intimated that he'd come back for someone and suggested it was you. Maybe she got it wrong and there's something else.'

Georgie ground her molars. There was certainly no girlfriend in Glengarrick. Maybe she should tell Nick to take his search back to Geelong and look for the secret girlfriend she'd overheard the women gossiping about earlier.

'Jed's just back in town to toss the coin,' Georgie said, keeping her tone even and trying to be polite. There was nothing to gain by giving Nick cause to ask more questions. 'I'm sure when he decides what he's going to do next in terms of his career, you'll be the first person he calls.' She smiled sweetly. 'As for his personal life?' She offered an offhand shrug. 'Jed's always kept that private.'

'Oh, well, if you change your mind and you think of something you want to tell me about Jed, or even if you want to chat, will you call me?' He pulled out a wallet, extracted a business card and held it out to them. 'Here's my number. Call me,' he repeated. 'Any time.'

Zara refused to take his card. 'If you'll excuse us, we need to find a spot to watch the game. I suggest you do the same thing and don't go bothering people for information on Jed. It's not about him today, it's about the Glengarrick Football Club.'

Zara flounced off, dragging Georgie by the elbow. Georgie had to jog to catch up. She was cross, but not as annoyed as Zara clearly was.

'What an arrogant so and so,' Zara said with a huff. 'Guys like him give journalists a bad name.'

'He had some nerve,' Georgie agreed, once they'd found a vacant spot on the boundary. There was still nearly an hour before the first bounce and not many people were ready to find a place to sit or stand yet.

'I wonder who he spoke to?' Zara asked. 'Who would have said you two had a thing?'

'I have no idea, but clearly someone thinks we do—did— urgh…did you hear those old women at the cake stall? They said Jed has a girlfriend in Geelong. And that I'm out of his league.' The words stung.

Zara scowled. 'Ignore them. And no. If Jed has a girlfriend, he would have said something last night. He wouldn't lie. Jed was always trustworthy at school, and from what I know of him, that hasn't changed. I know you haven't seen him since school, but he and I have caught up now and then for a drink when I've been in Geelong, and he's always been a man of character and integrity.'

Georgie frowned. 'I didn't know you'd seen him.'

'Once or twice. Anyway, Jed's built his entire football career on his impeccable record both on and off the field. If there was a woman in his life, we'd have heard about her because he would have told us.'

Georgie nodded. 'You're right.' A sudden thought slammed into her. She put her hands to her flaming cheeks. 'Crap, crap, crap!'

'What?' Zara stared at her.

Michelle.

When Jed's mum got home last night from helping down at the SES headquarters, she would have realised Georgie had slept in Jed's bed, not the spare room. Georgie's stomach knotted. Had Michelle said something to Nick. Was she telling people Georgie and Jed were an item? She needed to find Jed and talk to him.

'George?' Zara was still staring at her, waiting for her to explain.

'Sorry. Argh. I know where Nick got his information. I stayed at Jed's last night.'

Zara's eyes widened then a grin broke out across her face. 'Go girl.'

'It's not what you think,' she replied hastily. 'A tree fell and blocked the road back to my place and we couldn't get through. He offered for me to stay at his place. I slept in the spare room,' she lied.

Zara's face fell. 'Bummer.'

'Michelle must have just presumed we slept together.' Michelle would have known they'd slept together when she saw the still unmade bed in the spare room.

'So, there's nothing between you guys?'

Georgie shrugged. She wasn't actually sure. Technically whatever last night was, it wasn't a one-night stand because if you slept with the same guy twice, you couldn't call it that, could you? Perhaps last night had merely been a re-enactment of the night of the storm. Or it had been nothing.

She sighed softly. She had so many questions. Ones only Jed could answer.

Chapter 14

Jed always got to the ground early on game day. He liked to be the first one in the team's rooms because he loved savouring the time of calmness and clarity before everything went into hyped overdrive. Even on a day like today—the Murray Valley Football League's Grand Final—when he wasn't even playing, he'd arrived earlier than he needed to.

He'd received a text message from Frank Deltondo, the coach, checking to make sure he was ready for his big moment. Jed had tried not to laugh as he replied to the text. Tossing the coin was hardly a big moment in his career but he understood Frank was keen for Jed to encourage some of the younger players that they could hit the big league if they wanted it badly enough.

Jed wasn't surprised when he got to the Glengarrick Saints Football and Netball Club grounds and found two players already in the rooms. They sat on the floor at the far end of the large open space, their backs against the cream-coloured cinder brick wall. Both wore noise cancelling headphones. Jed gave them a wave and they waved back, but neither of them removed their headphones. He didn't take offence. They were in the zone.

He was in the zone too. The zone where he couldn't get Georgie out of his head. He still wasn't sure if they'd made the biggest mistake ever by sleeping together last night or whether it was his best move yet. Having her fall asleep spooned in his arms had felt better than winning a premiership. This morning he'd woken and still felt like he was walking ten feet off the ground.

He'd had his share of relationships over the past ten years, but they had been casual arrangements where both parties knew the rules, and nobody got hurt. But Georgie was different. He didn't want to do anything to hurt her. Problem was, he'd already slept with her once and walked away.

His future was so up in the air. His agent had texted to say he was currently talking to two clubs about an assistant coaching role. If he got one of them, he'd be leaving Glengarrick—and Georgie—again. If he left and returned, he couldn't expect her to fall back into his arms a second time.

He pushed the thoughts aside. Now wasn't the time to be thinking about Georgie and the future. He needed to concentrate on the present.

He stopped at the small anteroom which in his day had doubled as a storeroom and the room where the physio crammed in her portable table and players got taped up before the game. Today, it was a different room. A window had been installed and from the desk in front of the window, the entire ground could be viewed. It was well-lit and freshly painted in black, red, and white stripes—the teams' colours. An examination table took up most of the space. Next to the desk was an open shelf containing bandages and tapes and, on the desk, sat a flat screen TV. He was impressed. The club had come a long way in ten years. No doubt a physio could sit in the room and watch the game in real time as well as watch it streamed so they could see close ups of any contests that might result in injuries.

Being in the rooms brought back memories of the years he'd played for the club: the sights, the sounds. Mostly the smells. No amount of fresh air ever got rid of the smell of menthol, sweat and mud.

There was still an hour or so until the game began and the hum of noise in the locker room was growing to a loud buzz. Over the scratchy tannoy system, someone blared out instructions about parking and where to buy pre-game food and drinks. A siren sounded, signalling the beginning or end—Jed wasn't sure—of the netball final on the adjoining courts.

'Jed.'

He turned to see Frank striding towards him, hand outstretched.

'So good you could make it.'

Frank was a stalwart of the club. Jed couldn't remember but he had a feeling this was Frank's fifteenth year as coach. It wasn't that no-one else wanted the job, no-one else in town was good enough to take over Frank's reins. Frank had to be approaching seventy, but he was still fitter than most men half his age.

'How ya doin?' he asked, slapping Jed on the back after they shook hands. 'Good to be back?'

Jed nodded. 'It's been a great weekend so far.'

'You hear about our girls?'

Jed shook his head. Yesterday the women's team had played their own Grand Final in Wangaratta.

'First year playing in the MVFL and they won. Bloody amazing.'

'Fantastic.' Jed was a huge supporter of women's football. Annabel, one of his best friends, was the ruck for the Geelong women's team.

'It's what our boys need. They'll be pumped.'

A player entered the room and as he walked past, Frank slapped him on the back. 'Good on ya, Robbo.' He turned back to Jed. 'Captain of the side two years running. Top player. Not as good as you though.'

Jed laughed. They emerged from the twilight of the rooms and Jed was taken aback by the noise and sheer enormity of the crowd. It looked like the entire town and a good portion of the population of surrounding towns had shown up.

'Bit different from your day, isn't it?' Frank asked.

'They never had pre-game entertainment when I played.' The

band wasn't that great, but they were providing atmosphere, which was all that mattered.

Banners at either end of the ground were being prepared, ready for the players to run through. There hadn't been banners ten years ago.

Despite having played in front of huge crowds at the Melbourne Cricket Ground, Jed's pulse quickened.

Frank picked up on it. 'You wish you were playing?'

'Yeah.' More than anything.

'After you've done the toss, you want to sit with me in the box?'

When he'd dropped Georgie back to her place earlier that morning after breakfast, she'd asked him where he'd planned to watch the game. He'd told her he'd find her and sit with her and the others, but perhaps it would be a better option to stay in the box. That way people would stay focused on the game, not him.

'I might hang with you for the first half then go and find my friends.'

'Suit yourself.'

The coin toss went off without a hitch or any fuss. Jed had half-expected Channel Seven to send a journalist or a cameraman, but they didn't. At least not that he'd noticed. There were a few cameras, but he hadn't spotted the familiar red and white logo. He put the media out of his mind and focused on the players as they ran through the banners and began their warmup sprints. There was no reason why anyone would bother following him back home. It wasn't like he was top news anymore and tossing a coin was hardly newsworthy.

After the opening siren, Jed held his breath as the umpire bounced the ball and the two rucks jostled for position, knees and shins smacking into each other as they jumped into the air to be the first to tap the ball out of the centre.

Moments later there was an even harder collision involving three players. Frank jumped to his feet swearing, then cheered and clapped when the Saints player spun out of it and kept running, seemingly unaffected. Number seven for the Saints got the ball and ran with it, but his run didn't last long before he was surrounded by opposition players and forced to kick into open space.

Jed couldn't help but notice that the opposition—the Wodonga Rovers—appeared faster and smoother than the Saints, but he kept that to himself. He'd heard complaints that the Rovers had had a less bruising season than Glengarrick and they were expected to win this game easily. Even so, there was fight in the Saints, and as Jed's coach at Geelong had said on many occasions: "it ain't over till the fat lady sings."

Five minutes into the first quarter the Saint's ruckman came limping off after a particularly violent collision. It was a rough and tough game, made worse by the awful condition of the ground. Saturday's storm had turned the centre into a slippery mud bath.

'Bloody old knees.' Frank said, keeping his eyes fixed on the game in front of him. 'Fraser's thirty next year. Too old. Should be playing Masters, not Seniors level, but we don't have any other up and coming rucks.'

Jed kept quiet. *He* was thirty next year and if it hadn't been for the concussion injury, he'd still be playing. When he'd played, his own knees often caused him pain, but not enough to force him of the ground. He coped because of the flow of adrenalin surging through his body. Afterwards he could barely walk, but he never admitted that.

Fraser hobbled past, flanked by two women, each wearing hot pink high vis vests. One bore the title "Physio", the other "Nurse".

'How bad's the pain, from one to ten?' Frank called out.

'Two,' Fraser said, grey and thin-lipped. Jed recognised that look. He glanced at Frank to see if Frank believed him.

Frank shrugged. 'They'll check him out and strap him up. He'll be good to go after a quick break. He's also the local doctor and knows how hard he can push his body.' He fixed his attention back on the play.

Jed glanced up at the scoreboard; in the time it took for Fraser to come off, the other team had kicked a goal and were up by two.

For the rest of the quarter, activity around the coaching box and interchange bench was frenetic and chaotic. Frank wasn't the kind of coach to yell, but others were doing his share of shouting— calling out the calm instructions he delivered to them and passing them onto the players.

'Get Henley back on, send him back on now!'

'Get a runner out there, we need Jacko to fall back and cover their loose man.'

Jed turned his attention back to the game. A hard clash of bodies sent two players to the ground and Jed's pulse spiked. When they both got to their feet, he exhaled. Was this how Georgie and Mum felt, watching him play?

One of the Saints' players got pinned to the ground holding the ball and the umpire blew his whistle. The player clambered out of the scrum and dusted himself off. Unhurt, or anaesthetised by adrenalin—or both. The ball came down and was quickly kicked into the forward half, with Saints and Rover players streaming after it.

Behind Jed, Frank cheered when number nine—a kid who couldn't be much older than seventeen—ran in front of the pack and got into the forward fifty. He took a high mark and didn't stop running until he was five metres from the goal, where he kicked high and long. And straight through the middle of the posts.

Jed gave a reflex shout of approval as did the entire crowd. Everyone stood and cheered, and car horns blared and tooted to acknowledge Glengarrick's first goal of the game.

Frank slapped his thigh. 'We need another one quick out of the middle, quick out of the middle.'

In the muddy centre square, the ball was bounced but it veered off and the umpire brought it back and threw it high in the air, so the ruckmen had to focus on the vertical leap. Fraser got to it first, tapping the ball out. On the ground, a writhing mass of players dove into the mud, fighting for the ball. One of the Rovers broke free and the Saint's forward reached out to stop him, but the player's size and momentum was too much. The Saint's arm twisted back behind his body awkwardly. He instantly hunched over in a protective pose, bent almost double as he cradled his arm. The shoulder was clearly dislocated.

When the nurse ran out on the field and brought him back to the sidelines the noise of the crowd instantly amplified. Jed's own pulse galloped.

'You'll be right, mate,' Frank said as the player walked past, clutching his forearm and sucking air through his teeth. 'Doc'll fix you up.'

'Yeah, but I'm out for the rest of the game,' the player growled.

Jed felt the guy's pain. Being told he couldn't go back on the field was a kick in the guts he well knew. He had no doubt this player, like most of the boys, would downplay his injury, calling it a "niggle".

When the three quarter-time siren sounded, Jed checked the scoreboard. Surprisingly, the Rovers were only three points ahead. During the final break, while Frank went out onto the ground to talk to the players one last time, Jed left the coach's box in search of Georgie or any of the other guys from school. He saw Jack and

Emma, but they said they hadn't seen the others.

He wandered around the outside of the oval, surprised no-one stopped him. A few people who noticed him, smiled in recognition, but today was all about the Saints. He found a gap in the crowd near the fence on the wing and positioned himself there. Frank wouldn't care that he didn't sit out the rest of the game in the box. He sent Georgie a quick message letting her know where he was, in case she was looking for him. There had to be at least a thousand people circling the oval up to three people deep in some places.

The siren sounded for the start of the final quarter. Jed was beginning to think the game had done its worst in terms of injuries when an opposition player jumped for a contested mark and took an elbow directly to his temple. A gasp echoed around the ground. He went down heavily at an awkward angle, not putting his hands out to break his fall and was unconscious before he reached the ground. Within seconds though, he clumsily attempted to sit up, looking dazed and confused, clearly concussed. One of the runners helped him to his feet and walked him off the ground. Jed shook his head. He wouldn't be coming back on.

'Bringing back memories?' a soft voice asked.

He turned to see Georgie at his side. His pulse quickened and it took all his willpower not to take her into his arms and kiss her. But he couldn't do that until he knew what last night had meant to her. Neither of them had said much about the future when he dropped her back to her car down at the river that morning.

'You got my text?' he asked.

She nodded. 'I was wondering where you were.'

'Sorry. Frank asked me to sit in the box and watch.'

'I figured that's what happened. I watched you toss the coin, then you were gone.'

They stood side by side watching the game mostly in silence.

'It's a tough match,' she said after a while.

'Very tough. The ground is so wet after all the rain we had yesterday. They'll be stuffed tonight.'

'I can't believe how many injuries there have been.'

It was clear Frank had told the players to dial up the intensity. Saints players were tackling everyone, desperately scrambling after the ball. One player scored a knee to the abdomen but got straight back up and kept running. A similar contact on another player, this time an elbow to the stomach. He played on too, not even glancing at the interchange bench. The Saints were down by five points. Players had to be chased by runners to make them leave the ground. Jed knew what that felt like. When a game was this close, no-one wanted to be off the ground for even a minute.

Jed checked the scoreboard. Thirty-one minutes. Depending on how much overtime there was, if the Saints could get the ball out of the centre and kick a goal, they'd win. The noise of the crowd was insane, filling his head. He shifted his weight from one leg to the other, then gripped the cold metal rail. Every cell of his being wished he was out there playing.

Georgie glanced at him before reaching over and putting her hand on his. 'It takes guts to show up here so soon after your retirement. I think you're incredibly brave.'

He glanced down at her. 'Thanks, Georgie.'

He didn't feel brave. Right now, he felt angry. Cheated. Frustrated. Confused.

'Don't let your feelings drive you, Jed.'

Was she reading his mind?

He pushed away from the fence and was about to say something when a scrum near the boundary stopped play for a moment, taking his attention away from Georgie and back to the game. A Saints player got the ball and kept it clear, fighting his way into a gap. He kicked the ball towards the Saint's end and the noise around the ground reached a pitch that didn't seem possible in such a small place.

The ball was marked, and the player spun around, kicking off his left boot. It soared high over the posts and for a moment no-one knew if he'd scored a goal or a behind. As the siren sounded, the umpire gave the signal.

Goal.

The Saints had won.

Jed celebrated by lifting Georgie off her feet, spinning her around and kissing her firmly on the lips, not caring who was watching.

Judging by the way she returned his kiss she didn't care either.

Chapter 15

Later that night Georgie got out of her car and tugged at the low neckline of her slim-fitting dress. In rarely worn heels she hobbled across the road towards Zara who stood outside the pub waiting for her. How had she let Zara talk her into this? She'd always enjoyed singing, but it was something she hadn't done since high school. This year though, Zara's parents had come up with the idea of a karaoke night to coincide with the run as a fundraiser for the football club. Knowing that made it harder for Georgie to bow out.

The music coming from inside was muffled, but Georgie recognised the Saints theme song and smiled. Perhaps it wouldn't be such a bad night after all. The entire town would be in great spirits after celebrating an incredibly close win against the Rovers. And Jed would be there which was her main reason for agreeing to come.

Georgie's lips still tingled from his kiss after the final siren sounded. There was no way he had a girlfriend. If he did, he never would have kissed Georgie in public. The world was too small.

Someone might have seen them kiss and taken a photo. All it would take was for them to upload it to social media and tag Jed in it. A chill ran through her. What if Nick, the journalist, had seen them kiss and he made up a story about her and Jed?

'Stop it,' Zara ordered after she pulled at the neck of the dress again. 'You look hot. You have the boobs, show them off. If you keep pulling your dress up, you'll ruin the effect.'

'What effect?'

'The I'm-here-to-have-a-good-time effect.'

Georgie rolled her eyes. 'I don't think so.

'Loosen up, George. You're behaving like a nana. It's time you lived a little and stopped working yourself to death.'

'Easy for you to say. You don't have the stress of running your own business.' Or the stress of dealing with a parent with mental health issues.

'Which is why I want you to put that out of your mind and have fun tonight, okay? It's been a great weekend and I have to head back to Melbourne tomorrow morning so let's go out with a bang. All the gang will be here, so we'll have a few bevvies, sing a bit, maybe dance. It'll be great.'

'I'm not letting you get me drunk,' Georgie said. 'I still feel sick when I remember how I felt the day after your twenty-first.'

Zara laughed. 'Yeah, that was a bit wild. But tonight, will be fun and you're entitled to a good time. Now come here so I can fix your dress again.'

Zara reached over and pulled Georgie's dress down, revealing more cleavage than Georgie was comfortable showing off.

Laughing, she smacked Zara's hands away and pulled the dress back up. 'Stop it. You're acting like I'm here to pick up.'

And she definitely was *not*.

She'd seen it happen every year. People came from miles away with the intention of getting laid. Perhaps she should warn Jed to be careful in case some woman got the wrong idea. Not that he was hers, but she wasn't letting someone else get their hands on him.

Georgie pushed the door open and they walked in. The beat of the music hit her like a wave, pulsing through her body and making her smile. Whoever the DJ was, he had good taste in song choices. Zara was right. It had been a long time since Georgie had really let her hair down.

'Grab us a table,' Zara ordered, 'while I get drinks.'

Georgie headed towards the back of the pub, as far away from the small stage as she could. They were early and the pub was only half full. By the end of the night, it would be standing room only. With any luck, Zara would forget about the whole karaoke thing.

She pulled out a chair and was about to sit when someone put a hand on her back. She stiffened, spun around, then relaxed.

'Come here often?' Jed drawled.

He draped an arm across her shoulders and her skin tingled. He was dressed in black jeans and a white shirt and looked incredible. When their gazes met, her heart skipped a beat, then another. How was she going to act like nothing had happened between them? Zara always said she was so easy to read and until she knew what was going on between them, she didn't want to have to answer questions from her friends.

'Ready for some singing?' he asked.

Her smile dropped a notch. She wasn't going to let Jed talk her into getting up there too. 'Did Zara put you up to this?'

'Nah.' He tilted his head towards the bar. 'Charlie.'

She looked over his shoulder and saw Zara and Charlie standing at the bar, not even trying to hide that they were watching them. Charlie gave her a thumbs up and she felt her face flush. She was so hyper-aware of Jed's presence she could barely concentrate. Either Jed didn't notice her reaction, or he pretended not to.

'Do they think they're trying to set us up?' she asked as she sat in the chair, angling it towards Jed's.

Jed grinned. 'Don't think we need their help, do we?'

She felt the blush spread.

Jed leaned in to say something and when his chest brushed against her shoulder, she jumped as if she'd been shocked. Under that shirt he was rock-hard muscle. Muscle that she'd enjoyed running her hands over last night.

'You look amazing, Georgie. I don't remember ever seeing you in such a sexy dress.'

'Thank you.' His compliment was exactly what she needed to

boost her confidence. 'Zara told me to dress up.'

'I'm glad you listened.'

When he put a hand on her bare thigh, her skin tingled.

'So, are we going to sing?' he asked.

She shook her head.

'Not even for old time's sake?' He grinned, and it all but broke her resolve.

'I haven't sung at all since school other than in the shower or at work when no-one's listening.'

'I'm sure you've still got it,' Jed replied.

Zara and Charlie headed their way, carrying drinks for everyone.

'Hey, Georgie Porgie. Lookin' smokin' in that dress,' Charlie said, before giving her a kiss on the cheek. 'It's going to be a great night.'

'I told her she deserved a night of fun,' Zara announced as if Georgie hadn't been out once in the past ten years.

The DJ announced he was taking requests for karaoke. Zara started to stand, but Georgie shook her head and gave Zara a pleading look. 'Not yet,' she mouthed.

Zara sat down again.

'How's things in Melbourne?' Jed asked Charlie.

'Alright. But to be honest, I'm thinking of coming back.'

'Really? To do what?' Georgie asked.

Like the others, Charlie had left town after school finished.

With a near perfect ATAR score, everyone presumed he'd do medicine, but instead he chose pharmacy. He always joked about avoiding the smart-Asian-kid-becoming-a-doctor stereotype. Charlie's mum was Chinese, and his dad was Caucasian.

'Ken's retiring and I'm thinking of buying the business,' Charlie said.

'That's awesome.' The old pharmacy needed an overhaul. 'You'd be perfect, and it would be so good to have you back here.'

'Good for you, mate,' Jed said.

'What about you, Jed?' Charlie asked, swivelling in his seat to face Jed. 'What are your plans now footy's finished.'

Jed shrugged. 'Still talking things through with my agent. There might be something coming up at one of the clubs in Melbourne.'

'Like a coaching role?' Charlie asked.

'Yeah. Maybe. Or player welfare. It's all up in the air.'

Georgie ventured a look at Jed. He didn't sound at all enthusiastic, although the others didn't seem to notice. Maybe she was reading something into it that wasn't there. For a moment, she got the feeling Jed was jealous of Charlie having something to come back to.

'How's your mum coping on the farm?' Charlie asked.

'Not great.' Jed sighed. 'So far she's refusing any financial help.'

'My folks are the same,' Charlie said. 'The rate Dad's going, they'll have to carry him off the farm in a pine box.' He turned to Georgie. 'What about your mum? How's she doing since your dad died?'

Georgie shifted in her seat and fiddled with her coaster. Charlie obviously hadn't heard about her mum's health struggles. At least that meant people in town weren't talking.

'She's as good as can be expected, I guess. Has good days and bad.' More bad days than good ones unfortunately. Georgie didn't usually like admitting how tough things were, but these were her friends. 'Unfortunately, it's been hard to convince her to get help. She needs a psychologist, but she won't go and see the GP to get a referral because she thinks he's too young. To be honest, I've given up telling her what to do.'

Charlie's eyes filled with concern. 'That's tough.'

Jed nodded. 'Yeah, that's got to be rough for you, Georgie.' He placed his hand on hers and squeezed briefly. 'I can kind of understand, because Mum went through something similar after Dad left, but I think her anger towards him is what kept her going.'

Wisely, no-one said a word about Jed's father. They all knew he was in a low-security prison doing ten years and Jed hadn't spoken to him since his sentencing. It had been all over the media.

Zara pushed back her chair and stood. 'I'm going to put my name on the karaoke list. Charlie, you up for it?'

Georgie smiled. Trust Zara to make sure the mood was lightened.

Charlie guffawed. 'Do you remember how bad I am?'

Georgie and Jed joined in his laughter.

'*I* remember,' Georgie said. 'You are the only person I know who is officially tone deaf.'

'Jed?' Zara asked. 'What about you?'

Jed rested his hand on Georgie's leg again, eyes full of question. This time the touch felt like an electric shock zapping her. 'Only if Georgie joins me for a duet.' He turned to face her. 'What do you say?'

Zara didn't wait to hear Georgie's answer. She dashed off.

'Go on,' Charlie said, sitting back in his chair with a grin. 'I still remember that song you two sang for *Glengarrick's Got Talent*. You guys were awesome.'

Georgie groaned, even though that night had been one of the highlights of her entire life so far. In costume as Disney's *Aladdin* and *Jasmine*, she and Jed had sung "A Whole New World" to thunderous applause and cheers from the entire town. Thank goodness no-one had filmed it. Jed would have been so embarrassed if a video of him had surfaced with him dressed in nothing except a pair of white harem pants and a purple vest. His fans—and the commentators of the footy shows—would have had had a field day.

'We weren't *that* good. Neither of us got a tap on the shoulder and cast in the next big musical,' she said.

'*I* was good,' Jed said earnestly, 'but you'— he gently touched her cheek and turned her face towards him, his thumb trailing down her jaw to her chin— '*you* were remarkable.'

He dropped his hand and they stared at each other. For a moment she forgot they were in the pub surrounded by people.

The intimate pause was broken by the DJ's voice. 'We have a treat for you tonight. First up is AFL superstar, Jed Delaney, and our very own Georgina Purcell, singing a duet.'

The crowd roared and Georgie froze. Could she do this? She glanced at Jed, but he didn't look at all perturbed. If anything, he looked amped.

Before she had a chance to run to the bathroom, Jed stood and grabbed her by the hand, gesturing towards the stage. 'Come on, George, it'll be fun. Like old times. Put a smile on and pretend you love the attention.'

She shot him a look that hopefully conveyed exactly how much "fun" she expected this to be, but all he did was laugh. Feigning reluctance, she allowed herself to be towed behind him towards the stage. Jed beamed like he was having the time of his life and it was hard not to get caught up in his enthusiasm. It was so infectious and his presence and faith in her was the boost she needed. When he leapt onto the stage and reached down to help her up, she took his outstretched hand and smiled up at him. She could do this. Besides, with everyone watching them, she'd look like a fool for turning Jed Delaney down.

'Thanks, Georgie,' he whispered in her ear as he handed her

one of the microphones.

He was so close, his warm breath tickled her neck and caused tingles of delight to race up and down her spine.

The music started and she laughed despite how nervous she felt. She'd figured Zara would ask the DJ to play the song from *Aladdin*, but instead, she'd picked an 80's classic: Human League's synthpop song, "Don't you want me". She glanced at Jed and he was laughing too.

'We got this,' he mouthed before leaning in close and pursing his lips in a mock-seductive kiss.

Jed clutched the microphone on the stand with both hands and started singing about meeting her in a cocktail bar. When he got to the next line about picking her out, shaking her up and turning her round, he let go of the microphone and scooped her up in his arms before dropping her down again and spinning her under his arm. He mucked up the next line, but the crowd didn't care. They went wild. Even Georgie couldn't stop giggling.

By the time she'd sung her verse and they made it to the second chorus, the entire pub was singing along with them, begging the question: "don't you want me, baby?".

Jed played the part perfectly, pretending to beg Georgie to give him another chance. In return, she teased and taunted him, coming close, then backing away, singing that she didn't need him. The crowd ate it up.

By the time they got to the final chorus, all Georgie's nerves were gone. She didn't even care that dozens of phones were pointed towards them, clearly videoing their performance. Even spotting Nick, the reporter from Channel Seven, didn't throw her off.

The song ended and they stood face to face, millimetres apart, breathing heavily from the exertion of their act. For a split second, Georgie felt like she was Lady Gaga, and Jed was Bradley Cooper and they'd just performed *Shallow* at the Oscars.

She looked up into Jed's eyes and couldn't stop herself. Reaching up, she brushed his cheek with the back of her hand. Their eyes stayed locked together as everyone cheered and clamoured for them to sing another song, but Georgie barely noticed. All she saw was the man before her, happy and at peace.

The man she'd fallen deeper in love with.

Her eyes travelled down to his lips, and her breath hitched. He leaned closer and for a moment she thought he was about to kiss her in front of everyone. A whistle from the audience snapped them both out of it and she took a step back and mentally shook her head. If she kissed Jed Delaney now, it would be all the morning talk show hosts would talk about.

Jed leaned into the microphone on the stand. 'Sorry, folks, that's all from us tonight. Guess you'll have to call us one hit wonders.'

He took her hand and helped her down. Another couple took to the stage and another song started. Georgie's legs shook as they walked back to the table hand-in-hand, but she couldn't deny how much fun she'd had.

Charlie and Zara stared at them, mouths agape.

'That was incredible. Outstanding. Just…wow,' Zara gushed.

'I don't remember them teaching that kind of chemistry at high school,' Charlie said. 'Anyone would think you two have something going on.'

Georgie felt the heat on her cheeks and hoped her friends would think she was just flushed from her performance.

'The question is,' Zara said, staring from Georgie to Jed, 'what are you going to do about it?'

Ignoring Zara's question, Georgie downed a glass of water and hoped someone else would change the subject. Jed offered to get them another round of drinks and something to eat and the conversation moved on.

The pub buzzed, the karaoke continued and for the next hour the four of them sat at the table talking and enjoying each other's company and scoring the other singers. Georgie had to secretly admit if it were a competition, she and Jed would have won.

But, as much as she was having a great night, Georgie was a working girl and she had a café to open early tomorrow morning. By ten-thirty, the big weekend had caught up with her. Stifling her third yawn in five minutes, she pushed her empty water glass away. 'Time for me to hit the road, I reckon. It's getting late.'

'It's not even eleven o'clock,' Zara said.

'Been a big weekend,' Jed said. 'I might head off too.'

'We'll have to get together again soon,' Charlie suggested. 'Have dinner with everyone. Maybe you could come down to Melbourne, Georgie.'

'Definitely,' Georgie agreed. 'And you'll have to let me know what happens with the pharmacy.'

'Absolutely. How much longer are you staying in town, Jed?' Charlie asked. 'Are you hanging around or will you head back to Melbourne tomorrow?'

Jed stilled. 'I…I'm not sure. Guess it will depend on what my agent says. I'm waiting for him to call.'

A flicker of insecurity went through Georgie. She shot Jed a look. What *were* his plans if the assistant coaching job didn't come off? Would he consider staying? If he did, what did that mean for them?

'Ready to go, George?' Jed's voice brought her back to the present.

She pushed her doubts aside. There was no point worrying about a future with Jed when she had no idea what their "present" looked like. They'd spent one night together. Okay, two, but she wasn't sure she should count that first night because it was so long ago.

Last night was wonderful, but she didn't know if what she had with Jed would amount to anything. It was still too fresh to give it an official title. Best thing to do was bask in the memory of it and save the questions about the future for later. With any luck, they'd spend tonight together and tomorrow they could talk about what was next.

'You still didn't answer my question,' Zara said. 'Whatever it is between you two, what are you going to do about it?'

Jed put an arm around Georgie's shoulder and hugged her. The close contact of his body against hers, pressing into her, reminded her of lying next to him in bed. She felt her face flame again and was glad it was dark in the pub and Zara couldn't see her face.

'I'll tell you what we're going to do about it,' Jed said. 'Tomorrow night I'm cooking her dinner.'

Georgie glanced up at him in surprise. 'You are?' That was the last thing she'd expected to hear him say.

Chapter 16

'I hope you don't have any plans tomorrow night,' Jed said, as they stood, shivering, outside the pub ten minutes later.

Georgie shook her head. The café was closed on Mondays and Monday nights were for chilling at home with Netflix for company. 'No plans. But you don't have to cook dinner for me.'

'I'd like to but…'

When he hesitated, disappointment surged through her. Georgie was about to give him an easy way to back out when he kept talking.

'It's a bit awkward asking Mum to go out for the night, that's all.'

'Oh, yeah.' Why hadn't she thought of that?

He chuckled. 'Who would have thought we'd be about to turn thirty and still living at home with our mothers?'

'Definitely not me.' As much as it was nice that Jed was making an attempt to understand what her life was like still living at home with her mother, it was hard to hold back the embarrassment that her life wasn't a little bigger and more exciting. She could only imagine what Jed's social calendar must be like.

'Would it be weird if we had dinner at the café? You can say no, and we could go to the Indian place, but it wouldn't be private.'

'Not at all weird. That's a great idea. I can help you cook.'

'Deal.' He grinned. 'You hungry now? We could see if it's not too late to order a pizza.'

She shook her head. 'I'm not that hungry, sorry.'

'Bummer. I could eat a horse.'

She giggled. 'Do you always think about your stomach?'

'Yeah. Pretty much.' He grinned then his smile changed and the look on his face became serious. 'Hey…ah…thanks for a great night tonight. I really enjoyed myself.'

She tilted her head and looked up at him. 'And what about last night? Did you enjoy that?' The teasing questions were past her lips before she could stop them. She glanced at her feet. How awkward. He probably thought she was fishing for a compliment of how good she was in bed.

'Oh, trust me George,' he replied huskily. 'Last night was beyond great.'

She looked back up. He was grinning at her and a wave of warmth swept over her. 'It's been a really good weekend,' she agreed lamely.

'I think that's the understatement of the decade.'

If only they could have a repeat performance of last night, but as Jed had just pointed out, the issue of living at home with their mothers was problematic. They were both too old to be sneaking into their own houses and hoping their mothers didn't hear them.

'I think your mum knows we slept together last night,' she said.

He frowned. 'What makes you say that?'

She told him about her conversation with Nick.

'I know the guy. He's always fishing for information. Don't give it another thought.'

'You're not worried your mum thinks we're sleeping together?'

He grinned. 'Not at all.'

Relief rushed in. 'Okay. So, I'll meet you tomorrow at the café around six. Does that work for you?'

He pushed back her hair. 'Works for me.' His eyes, dark with desire, met hers. 'All of a sudden I'm no longer hungry.'

'Really? That horse will be happy to know it's going to live another day.'

He leaned in and whispered in her ear. 'I don't need food. I need you.'

Jed tilted her chin back and his fingers tangled in her hair, tugging at the tie, until her hair cascaded around her shoulders. Warmth flooded her as he lowered his head and caught her mouth in his. His lips were warm, tasting slightly of beer and the promise of further intimacy. Within seconds their kiss blossomed into something much more. The intensity of Georgie's desire shocked her, but she wasn't about to stop to work out what was going on in her head. She wanted him. She needed him.

He stroked her cheek with one finger as though he was curious whether she still felt the same. It seemed longer than a day since they'd last been intimate and she hadn't realised how much she'd missed his soft touch. Her skin tingled as he slowly traced her cheekbone, her nose, the outline of her lips. Blood rushed around her body, waking her up again.

'You're so beautiful, Georgie.'

She closed her eyes and parted her lips. His finger traced down her neck, along the scoop of her shoulder to the hollow of her throat. Streams of heat zipped through her, weakening her arms, and loosening her legs. He knew exactly where to touch her to bring pleasure.

She closed the gap between them and felt his body respond as he pulled her to him. She ran her hand down his back, across his hip and felt the tightness of his buttocks under the fabric of his jeans. Their eyes locked, and they swayed slightly in each other's arms before their lips met in another tender kiss. She moaned softly.

'Damn, Georgie,' he murmured against her lips. 'You're killing me.'

She was about to suggest they drive to Stockton and get a

hotel room when his phone rang.

He pulled it from his pocket and a frown creased his brow. 'There's been a few missed calls. I mustn't have heard it in the pub.'

She frowned. 'At eleven o'clock at night?'

'Sorry, I need to take it. It's my agent. Hello? Hey, Chris, how are you?' He moved away from her. 'Oh, really? They want me? That's awesome. Yeah, I'll think about it, but I reckon you know my answer. I'll let you know for sure tomorrow.'

When he hung up and looked at her, his eyes shone. 'The Bombers want to chat to me about coming on as an assistant coach starting straight away.'

Georgie's heart dropped from her chest to her stomach. She should have known Jed wouldn't stick around. Shouldn't have let the last forty-eight hours go to her head. Grabbing her car keys, she headed for her car. Jed walked beside her, and it wasn't her imagination that there was an extra spring in his step.

She struggled to swallow past the lump in the back of her throat. It couldn't be happening again. She'd let herself get close to him and he was going to leave.

Forcing a smile, she said, 'That's...that's so good, Jed.' Her voice sounded thick to her ears, but Jed didn't seem to notice. 'Of course, you have to take it. You'd be crazy not to. What an opportunity.'

All she wanted to do was lay her head on his chest and feel his strong arms around her and hear him say he was turning down the offer and staying with her.

She didn't want to say goodbye to him. Not again. Didn't want Jed, who'd breezed into her life and made her smile again, to breeze out. But it looked like he was going to, and she needed to let him go.

'You know, Jed, that game last month where you got concussed the second time…everyone was hoping and praying you'd make another comeback like you did earlier in the year. I wanted that for you too. But more than that, when I watched you go down, all I hoped and prayed was you'd get up and be okay. When I knew you were alright, all that mattered was you'd be happy. So, this coaching gig...I really hope it makes you happy.' Her face felt like it was about to crack under the strain of trying to keep the smile fixed there.

'Oh, Georgie, I'm sorry.'

His voice was so serious, but the finality in his tone hit directly at her weakened reserves. She wished she hadn't said anything. She bit her bottom lip to stem the tears.

'It's probably best if we give dinner tomorrow a miss,' she said.

'Yeah. Probably.'

There was a tiny awkward moment as he stared at her. What should she do? Shake his hand? Get in her car and give him a casual wave as she drove away?

Kiss…?

Jed answered the next question before it had even fully formed. Pulling her towards him, he held her for a moment, her chest pressing against his, until he moved away just enough to place his hand on her shoulders.

His kiss was aimed at her cheek, but she moved too quickly, and his lips grazed hers for less than a second. The familiar soft warmth of his mouth on hers was as unexpected as it was welcome. Georgie swallowed hard and pulled away, biting back fresh hot tears, and pushing away unwelcome stirrings and disappointment. Why did this feel like a permanent goodbye?

He squeezed her shoulder one last time. 'Take care, Georgie. Thanks again for an incredible weekend.'

Lips still burning from the brief touch, she unlocked her car door and he held it open while she got in and put the key in the ignition. What had she expected from one night together? That he would declare his undying love? He'd never indicated he'd intended to stay longer than the weekend and she'd let her emotions take off on her.

After closing the car door, she pressed the button to drop the window. Once he was back in Melbourne, she could go back to minding her own business, running the café, and pretending her life was great.

'You take care too, Jed.' She forced a smile. 'Essendon are lucky to have you and you'll be great.'

As she drove away, the tears fell. In the movies, breakups were usually big, dramatic scenes with shouting and weeping, begging and rejection. But that wasn't how it worked.

Breaking hearts didn't make a sound.

Chapter 17

After the weekend, the town buzzed for days with everyone stopping in the street to chat about the Saints men's and women's teams winning the Grand Final. The café was blessedly busy, which thankfully left Georgie little time to think about Jed. But by Friday afternoon, when the streets were empty and life had resumed its normal snail's pace, a foggy feeling settled over her. She was miserable. She missed her friends, especially Zara. It had been so much fun having everyone around for the weekend and now they were gone, back to their lives. It even looked like Charlie might not be moving back with the sale of the pharmacy possibly not going ahead.

Mostly, she missed Jed.

Saying goodbye that night had been hell. She'd hoped she might see him again before he left town, but he was gone the next morning. All she'd got was a text thanking her again for a great weekend and saying he'd chat to her soon. As if their night together had meant zilch.

During the week she'd foolishly done some social media checking, even though she knew Jed's accounts were basically inactive. Most of his photos were of beach scenes, photos of coffee or reposted photos from the footy club's official site.

As she expected, he hadn't posted anything—not even a photo of him tossing the coin. It was almost as if the weekend hadn't happened.

However, a grainy video had surfaced on YouTube of their karaoke performance. When she didn't hear from Jed, she wondered if he'd even seen it. At least whoever took the video had stopped recording when they finished singing. It would have been impossible to deny the chemistry between them during the last few moments of the song as the music ended.

Georgie exhaled heavily. She was carrying on like he'd broken off their engagement instead of leaving town for a job. Her emotional attachment to him had to stop. Clearly, he'd been caught up in the nostalgia of being back in town and that's why he'd slept with her. She was so confused and wished she hadn't ended up in his bed again. All it had done was mess up everything.

As she'd spent time with him over the weekend, she'd realised how much she wanted to get to know him better. And now it was too late.

By the time she left work on Friday afternoon, Georgie wanted to crawl into bed and not come out again until Monday morning, but for Mum's sake she would put on a brave face. She was tired—

mentally, physically, and emotionally—but Mum didn't need to be burdened with that.

When she arrived home and saw her mum's car was gone, relief swept through her. She wasn't in the mood to talk. But that relief was followed quickly by a flicker of guilt. Mum didn't often leave the house, and when she did, it was usually to visit the cemetery. Although sometimes she drove into Stockton and wandered around the shops so perhaps that's where she was. She did that occasionally because no-one stopped to talk to her. Georgie forced herself to relax. If Mum was out and about, it meant today was a good day.

Inside, after getting changed out of her work clothes, she found a candle Zara had given her for her last birthday and lit that. Moments later, the sweet fragrance of vanilla and cinnamon wafted through the room, rekindling memories from her childhood and pushing back some of the heaviness in her heart. Her mum had loved to cook once, and the house always smelled like this: of freshly baked cakes, biscuits, and scones.

Georgie was opening windows to let in the fresh winter-nearly-spring air when she heard a car crunching on gravel. She glanced out the window. Mum was home.

But when Jane stepped through the front door, Georgie froze. Her mother's eyes were bloodshot as if she'd been crying.

She took two steps forward and opened her arms. 'I'm sorry, Georgie,' she whispered. 'I'm so, so sorry.'

Georgie's heart stalled for a second before she went to Mum and hugged her tight. She wanted to say it was okay, but it wasn't. It hadn't been okay for far too long. Instead, she asked, 'Is everything alright? Do you want to talk?'

Mum shook her head. 'No. I've had enough talking.'

Georgie held her tongue. They hadn't talked properly in a long time and that's exactly what they should be doing. They needed to clear the air and come up with a plan to move forward. 'I'll get dinner then,' she muttered.

Mum caught her wrist. 'I'm sorry, darling, that came out wrong. I'm happy to talk—I want to—about Dad, about us. But not tonight, okay? Tonight, I want to talk about you. I heard Jed Delaney was back in town last weekend. Did you see him?'

Georgie nodded, wondering where this was going.

'How was it seeing him again? You used to have a thing for him.'

Georgie exhaled slowly. 'I still do,' she murmured.

Mum's eyes widened.

'But I don't really want to talk about it.'

The breeze ruffled the curtains and Georgie turned to stare out at the view. Fluffy white clouds passed overhead and two cows eating grass along the fence line that bordered the house lifted their heads to stare back at her with dark eyes.

'Your Dad would have loved living here,' Mum said softly, coming to stand beside her at the window. Georgie was glad Mum didn't ask any more questions about Jed.

Out of nowhere, a fresh wave of grief washed over Georgie. She willed herself not to cry, but the tears, so close to the surface after an emotional week, trickled from her eyes and wouldn't stop. She let them flow, crying for Dad, Mum and all she'd lost. Crying for Jed and what might have been.

Mum took her hand and drew her outside into the bricked courtyard. Pulling out one of the chairs from the timber table they sat. Even though it was cold, the sun was out and there was no wind. Putting her feet up on another chair Georgie turned her face upwards, revelling in the sunshine and letting it dry her tears.

A magpie caw-cawed from one of the branches above her, before flying off, and somewhere in the distance was the low, steady hum of farm machinery.

Georgie exhaled slowly and steadily. 'Thanks. I needed this.' What she didn't need was the confusing feelings Jed had triggered in her.

'I think we both need this. Time and space and fresh air. It's good for the soul.'

Neither of them said anything for a while. In the silence Georgie tried to get her thoughts in order.

'What's going on, darling?' Mum asked eventually.

She wouldn't tell her mother she'd slept with Jed—that was too much information—but she would tell her about the weekend and how much it had affected her, seeing him again. She gave her mum a quick rundown.

'And now he's gone back to Melbourne,' she finished.

'If you feel this way about him, what's stopping you from following him?'

Georgie's head snapped up to look at her mother. Did she have to ask? 'Who would run the café if I went to Melbourne?'

The silence that fell was thick. It was the first time Georgie had given her mum any indication the café was a burden.

'Abbey could.'

She couldn't.

'I don't want to go to Melbourne, Mum. This is home. Glengarrick is where I want to be.'

'With Jed?'

Georgie shook her head. 'The sooner I let him go, the sooner I can get on with my life here.' She offered a weak smile.

'You could try internet dating?'

Georgie rolled her eyes. 'You're as bad as Zara.'

'Well, surely if women want to move to the country on that *Farmer Wants a Wife* television show, there must be some wonderful man out there for you who's dreaming of a country escape. You just have to find him.'

'I don't think it's that easy, Mum. Besides, internet dating is the last thing I want to do. It feels too clinical. As if I'm doing online shopping for a man.' She sighed. 'I think I need a holiday.' She couldn't remember the last time she'd been away longer than a weekend.

Mum leaned forward and put her hand on Georgie's arm. 'That's a wonderful idea. Why don't you get away for a few days? I'm sure Reece and Abbey are more than capable of running things, and if they get stuck I could…' Mum's voice trailed off.

They both knew Mum couldn't help. But Mum was right. Reece and Abbey could look after things for a week and they wouldn't need to bother Mum. The idea started to take root.

'I guess I could,' she said.

Knowing it could be a lot of pressure if she stayed at home with Mum, she'd book a house somewhere not far away. Maybe Beechworth or Bright. That way if something went wrong, she could be back home again in a few hours.

She reached for her mother's hand. 'I think I'll do that. Thank you.'

Mum smiled back. This time the silence between them wasn't as heavy.

'We really should do something about that lemon tree,' Mum said.

Georgie guiltily eyed the potted lemon tree the minister had given them at Dad's funeral. It was still in the original pot and its leaves were withered and dying.

'You remember he told us to plant it somewhere and nurture it and watch it grow?'

Georgie nodded. They'd bought it with them when they

moved here but had left it in its plastic pot. She didn't possess a green thumb, but she was confident she could re-pot a lemon tree without killing it. She looked around the courtyard. Perhaps she could weed the garden beds, too. It would give her something to do and keep her mind off Jed. "An idle mind is the devil's workshop" Dad used to say.

He would have also told her to stop wallowing and move on.

She stood. 'Want to give me a hand?'

***

An hour later, they stood and surveyed what they'd done.

Mum cupped her hand around Georgie's face. 'You got some sun this afternoon. You're glowing.'

'You look good too.'

Mum chuckled. 'It was good for my soul, but my back will probably tell me about it tomorrow.'

Georgie wrapped an arm around her mother's waist and rested her head on her chest. 'I'm glad we re-potted the lemon tree. I was worried it would die but didn't want to say anything to you and I was too worried to try to replant it myself in case I killed it.'

'Oh, darling.'

They held onto each other, as tears streamed down their faces. Despite the pain and loss and the depression and everything else that hovered unspoken over them for years, Georgie was at peace and she had a feeling Mum was too.

'I hope it grows,' Mum said after they'd wiped away their tears.

'It will.' Georgie was sure of it.

They stood until the sun sank over the horizon and a chill settled over them. As much as Georgie wanted to go inside and have a hot shower and get dinner sorted, she didn't want this precious moment to end.

'You must be starving,' she said finally.

'Famished.'

Georgie smiled. She couldn't remember the last time her mother had an appetite.

She took Georgie's hands and stared into her eyes. 'I love you, Georgie. I hope you know that.'

'I do.'

Chapter 18

Three weeks after leaving Glengarrick, Jed was driving home along the Great Ocean Road with Annabel Norton, the ruck for the Cats women's team beside him in the passenger seat. It had been a perfect spring day, bright and blue-skied—magic weather for a drive along the coast. In a few months, this stretch would be packed with holidaymakers but for now it seemed they had the road to themselves.

He and Annabel had become close friends after the club put them together for marketing purposes and he always enjoyed spending time with her. It worked for him, and Annabel, if people assumed they were a couple. Annabel protected him from random women approaching him, and he protected Annabel's under-the-radar relationship. She was seeing someone but needed to keep it under wraps until the guys' divorce went through.

They were on their way back to Geelong after spending the day at a school in the Otways. They'd been talking to a group of year nine students doing a rural residential program on a property owned by the school located outside of Lorne. The AFL had developed programs where players, or former players like Jed, went into schools to give motivational talks. It was something he'd always enjoyed, and when the school had called and asked if he and Annabel would come down together, he'd jumped at the chance. Partly to get out of Melbourne, partly to spend time with Annabel, and partly to clear his head and allow himself some thinking time and space.

The road wound through lush green rainforests, with the empty shore stretching out the left window. Although Jed loved the beach and loved the Great Ocean Road, he missed the wide-open paddocks around Glengarrick with the mountains in the background.

'What are your plans for summer?' Annabel asked as they approached Anglesea.

They'd spent the first bit of the drive unpacking how well the day had gone. Both agreed the students had gotten a lot out of what they'd had to say, especially the girls, who hero-worshipped Annabel. After today he wouldn't be surprised how many students switched from playing netball to footy.

'I haven't given much thought to next week, let alone summer,' he replied.

When he'd taken the job with the Bombers, Jed thought he'd be setting up an apartment in the city, hosting barbeques on his postage-stamp sized balcony overlooking Docklands and starting a new chapter of his life. Instead, every day he missed home a little more.

Whenever he thought about his future, it wasn't in Melbourne. He was on the farm. When he'd hastily left town not even out of his teens, he'd been too inexperienced and immature to realise what he'd lose by leaving. All it had taken was one long weekend back home, a fun run, the Grand Final and a night at the pub with everyone to wake him up. He'd felt a sense of community and belonging he'd only known when he played football. A feeling he never thought he'd have again. Glengarrick had somehow managed to wrap itself around him and it was refusing to let him go.

He missed Georgie too. After they'd made love, he'd been wrapped in a delicious haze of new beginnings and it had ended with a jolt. At the time it felt like they were at the start of something special, then he'd gotten the call from his agent. When Georgie urged him to accept the job he figured the feelings he had for her were one way and she'd seen him as nothing more than a bit of a fling. He scratched his chin. She *had* encouraged him to take the job, hadn't she? Or had he imagined it? The more he thought about it, the more he realised she hadn't been overly enthusiastic about the offer. Supportive, yes, the way any friend would be, but hardly jumping for joy. If he looked at it through her eyes, he'd accepted the job with seemingly zero thought about her or a potential future for them.

He'd left literally hours after making love to her and hadn't even called to see how she was. He'd only sent her one lousy text since he'd gone and the longer he went without calling her, the worse he felt. If he didn't do something soon, he'd be lucky if she ever spoke to him again. And he wouldn't blame her.

He was an idiot.

'The role at Essendon's not working out, is it?' Annabel asked, as if she somehow knew his swirling thoughts.

He exhaled softly and shook his head. 'You were right. I shouldn't have taken it, Bel.' It had only taken a week to realise he'd made the worst decision of his life. Being an assistant coach wasn't what he was supposed to be doing.

'Why did you? I said you shouldn't take it unless your heart was in it?'

He shrugged. 'I'm not sure I know the answer to that.'

'It's not like you need the money.'

'I figured it would keep me connected to the AFL.'

She nodded. 'That makes sense. But playing and coaching are two different things.'

'Yeah.'

'Are you on a contract?'

'Yes. Two years. I'm on three months' probation still.'

'Why don't you call your agent and tell him it isn't working.'

He glanced sideways at her. 'And do what?'

'For starters, go home. Clearly that's where you want to be. I don't know what happened when you were up there, but you haven't been the same since you came back. It's like your body is here and your mind is there.'

He sighed. 'If only it was that easy. Sure, I can go back to the farm, but if I do I could end up sitting around on my hands waiting for Mum to agree to let me take over from her.'

'You could go back to university.'

'And do what? I already have a degree.'

He had a Bachelor of Sports Science and was a qualified exercise physiologist but in the past ten years he hadn't put his degree to use.

'What about teaching? You come alive during these school programs. You were incredible today. The kids love you.'

'I guess.'

Silence filled the car. Could he do another two years of study to become a teacher? If he did, maybe he could turn the farm into a rural residential program like the one they'd just come from. Even without a teaching degree he could probably partner with a school and offer them the use of the property.

He kept his eyes on the road, but excitement mixed with hope—a feeling he hadn't experienced since retiring.

If he managed the business side of running the farm, he could get some of his AFL mates on board to act as mentors to the school kids. His mind sped with possibilities. The farm might be the perfect place for Georgie to run her camp for kids. It wouldn't be hard to build some basic accommodation.

Would it be crazy and impulsive to give up everything he had in Melbourne—a job, a place to live—for the unknown? Because if he went back, he'd have a seed of an idea and that's all. He wouldn't have a paid job and he might not even have Georgie.

After a long stretch of silence, Annabel put her hand on his arm. 'There's more to this than your job, isn't there?'

'Yeah.' He looked across at her. 'I feel like the biggest jerk. I walked away from someone special and I didn't leave well.'

'Does she know how you feel about her?'

'She knows,' he said, gripping the steering wheel tighter. 'But it makes no difference. I left her for a job. What does that say about me?'

There was a beat of silence.

'You probably don't want me to answer that,' Annabel said.

'It says my priorities are screwed.'

Annabel didn't reply. She didn't have to.

He rolled his neck to ease the kinks.

'How serious is it?' she asked.

'It could have been very serious if I hadn't stuffed it up.'

'Did you sleep with her?'

He sighed softly. 'Yeah, I did.' He and Annabel had always been honest with each other.

'And do you love her? Because I know you, Jed, and you're not a one-night stand kind of guy. I wouldn't have thought you'd kiss and move on.'

'Yet that's exactly what I did.'

He told Annabel almost everything—leaving out the personal details—starting from the night of the accident when he'd rescued Georgie right up to the Grand Final weekend. He even told her about being knocked out by the tree and how that could have changed the course of his entire life if Georgie hadn't kept his secret.

'Wow,' Annabel said when he'd finished.

'If only I hadn't taken the call from my agent,' he said.

'He would have called you the next day, so it makes no difference when the called. The question is: why did you accept the job when you didn't really want it? And why did you leave Georgie when you clearly love her?'

'I don't know.'

'Look at this from her point of view. If I were in her shoes, I'd be furious with you because it would look to me like you chose a job over a relationship.'

'Not once but twice,' he said. He scrubbed his face with a hand. 'What am I going to do?'

'Why do you need to ask? Call her.'

'And say what?'

Annabel groaned. 'Are you that stupid? Start with sorry, then tell her you love her.'

As if that statement ended the conversation and nothing else needed to be added, Annabel picked up her phone and started scrolling. She'd taken dozens of photos today and no doubt was uploading them to her social media account.

Suddenly she burst out laughing.

'What's so funny?'

'Since when did you take up karaoke?'

His heart went into double time. 'What?'

She held the phone up, but he didn't take his eyes off the road.

'You haven't seen this?'

'Seen what?' he asked, even though the moment he heard the opening notes of the song, he knew. Someone had videoed him and Georgie singing and posted it on YouTube.

When the music ended, Annabel whistled softly. 'Jeez, man, I'm going to take a stab that the woman in this video is Georgie.'

He nodded.

'How's the chemistry between you two?'

Fresh memories of the night came back. They'd had such a fun night until he ruined it.

'She can sing,' Annabel said, 'and you're not half-bad yourself.' She nudged him with her elbow before going back to the beginning of the clip to watch it again.

When the song ended a second time, Jed felt Annabel's gaze on him.

'What?' He glanced at her, then back at the road in front of them.

She waved her phone in the air. 'You need to watch this. It's obvious Georgie loves you. At the end of the song she looks at you the way Lady Gaga looked at Bradley Cooper.'

'Who?' He had no idea what Annabel was talking about.

'You need to watch *A Star is Born*. And you need to call her and tell her that you love her. As soon as you get home.'

For the next half hour they drove in silence, but Annabel's voice in his head was loud and insistent. She was right, he needed to call Georgie. Better still, he needed to get back to Glengarrick and see her in person and tell her he was sorry. If he was lucky, she'd give him another chance. If not, at least he'd tried.

When he pulled up outside Annabel's place in Geelong, he parked and shut off the engine.

'Thanks for a good day,' she said.

'Thanks for the chat.'

'Do you want to come in?' she asked.

He was momentarily torn. Stay and have dinner with Annabel and her boyfriend or go home to his empty apartment.

'Thanks, but I'll head home.' He had a lot more thinking to do.

Annabel hopped out of the car and came around to his side. He unwound the window.

'For what it's worth, I think you'd make an excellent teacher.'

'I'll think about it.'

'It's not a failure to quit the coaching job.' She put her hand on his arm and squeezed. 'And don't ignore the feelings you have for Georgie. I saw it in her eyes in that video. She might not know it yet, but she loves you.'

He turned to look at her. 'If only.'

Annabel smiled. 'There's one way to find out, Delaney. Go back home and talk to her before it's too late.'

Chapter 19

By the time Georgie finally got away from the café, it was late September. The last traces of winter were still clinging, but most of the days there was a promise of warmer weather ahead. It had been almost five weeks since she'd spoken to Jed. One text didn't count. He'd sent her a message with his new phone number and that was it. She'd replied, asking how the new job was going, but didn't hear back from him. She tried again a few days later. A friendly hi-how-are-you-doing text. He was probably flat out at work, but when she got no reply, it was hard not to feel rejected.

For her holiday she rented a small place outside Beechworth. She barely left the house for the first four days other than ducking into the supermarket for groceries and buying fish and chips one night for dinner. She pretty much slept for up to ten hours at a stretch and ate. She often found herself napping during the day as well, although she did manage to go for a run every morning to clear her head. It was as if seven years' worth of early morning starts at the café had finally caught up with her.

When she wasn't dozing on the couch, she took long baths in a tub that had views overlooking a secluded valley, read books and watched Netflix. She switched her phone to silent mode and promised herself not to get sucked down the rabbit hole of social media. The last thing she needed was to check Facebook or Instagram and see Jed's smiling face taunting her.

She'd foolishly started following Essendon's page and the announcement of Jed as the new assistant coach had been a kick in the ribs. She'd also seen photos of Jed with a woman called Annabel which probably explained why he hadn't replied to her texts. The mystery woman was no longer a mystery. He and the ruck of the women's team looked very chummy.

On her final day of self-imposed isolation, with no energy or desire to exert herself, she decided to go for a drive into town. Despite the amount of sleep she'd had this week, she was still bone weary.

After parking her car at the top of the main shopping strip, she wandered aimlessly down the street, stopping occasionally to peek into shops. She looked at clothes she couldn't be bothered trying on, at real estate she couldn't afford to purchase, and at restaurant menus advertising food she didn't want to eat. She ended up buying a ridiculously priced scented candle from the gift shop because it smelled too good to leave in the store even though she had dozens of candles at home.

She was heading back to her car when a photo in a gallery

window caught her attention. She paused to look at it. It was Geelong. Nostalgia and an unexpected sense of loss crept in. She'd been to Geelong a few times when she lived in Melbourne and she loved the waterfront city. Not that she'd ever have admitted it to anyone, but every time she'd visited, she hoped to randomly bump into Jed. But it was a large city and the chances of that happening were pretty slim and she never did.

The photo was large and set in a beautiful pale timber frame. It would look brilliant on the blank wall in the café. Artwork was the one thing she hadn't had time to think about. The price wasn't displayed, but she had a feeling she couldn't afford it. However, that didn't stop her from walking into the gallery anyway. There was no charge to look and there might be other smaller prints by the same photographer she could afford.

'Can I help you?' a male voice asked as soon as she entered.

She turned and stared at the man in front of her. He seemed vaguely familiar.

'Georgie Purcell.' He walked towards her, arms wide. 'Good to see you.'

She smiled and tried to place him.

'Pete Wilson, remember? We were at uni together. Friend of Neil's.'

'Of course. I didn't recognise you.' She accepted his friendly hug.

Neil had turned out to be a jerk, but Pete had been one of the nice guys. He looked a lot different from what she remembered—no longer sporting the scruffy just-been-surfing look, he wore navy chinos, leather lace ups and a buttoned-up white shirt. His beard was neatly trimmed and his hair short.

'I hope the fact you didn't recognise me is a good thing,' he said, chuckling. 'Because you look great.' He paused, as if he were about to say something else.

Please don't mention Neil.

Georgie cut him off. 'You look good too.'

An awkward silence fell.

'What are you doing in Beechworth?' Pete asked.

'Browsing. Relaxing. Not much really. You?'

'I live here.'

She frowned. 'Are you nursing up here?' Perhaps Pete was minding the gallery for someone.

He shook his head. 'Not now. You? I can't remember where you did your Grad year.'

'I didn't.'

'Oh?'

'My Dad got sick at the end of uni, and he died not long after that.'

'I'm sorry to hear that.'

She gave him a smile. Grief usually made others feel uncomfortable. 'I moved back home to help Mum and I haven't left.'

'Where's home?'

'Glengarrick. Near Stockton. I run a café called The Silver Spoon.'

'Nice part of the world. Cold in winter being so close to the ski fields.'

'It is,' she agreed. She gazed around the beautiful light-filled space. 'Speaking of nice, this gallery is gorgeous. I was walking past and saw the photo of Geelong in the window and I had to stop. Do you work here?'

'It's my gallery. My photographs. My artwork.' He held his hands out and she noted faint speckles of white on them. 'I paint too,' he said, pointing to a stunning piece of art she hadn't noticed. 'But I started out with photography. It pays the bills.'

'You're very talented. Why Geelong?'

'I lived there for five years. I did my Grad year at Epworth Hospital. Geelong's a great place to live.'

'I barrack for the Cats.' As soon as she blurted out the words, she wanted to take them back. What a stupid thing to say. What did Pete care which team she followed in the football?

Pete chuckled. 'I did too when I lived in Geelong. You kind of have to go for the Cats if you want to be accepted as a local.'

'Actually, I only went for them because I was at school with Jed Delaney. He's from Glengarrick.'

He raised his eyebrows. 'That's pretty cool. He was an amazing player and apparently a top bloke. You still friends?'

She wasn't sure how to answer that. Maybe. Maybe not. She had no idea what to call their relationship anymore. 'Yeah, we're friends.'

'Shame about his injury.'

'Yes, it is.' She needed to move the conversation away from Jed. 'I'm too scared to ask how much the photo in the window is. It would look great on the wall in my café.'

'A grand.'

Georgie winced. She'd expected it to be pricey, but nowhere close to that. 'Sadly, that doesn't fit into my budget.'

'Hang on for a minute okay,' Pete said before slipping out of sight between two rows of hanging art.

He returned moments later with a similar smaller version of the same photo in the window. It was on a matt background, unframed. 'I know it's different from the one in the window and not as big, but I'd like to give it to you.'

She shook her head. It was a lovely gesture, but Pete was being far too generous. 'I can't accept it but thank you anyway.'

'To be honest, it didn't develop properly.'

He indicated a small flaw she wouldn't have noticed unless he'd pointed it out.

'I want you to have it.' He gave her an apologetic look. 'As much as I'd love to give you the one in the window, I obviously can't. I have to eat this week.' He lifted a shoulder and grinned. 'You know how it is. Struggling artist and all that.'

Georgie tried to push the print back into his hands. 'I can't accept this, Pete, really I can't.'

'Consider it a good-to-see-you-again gift.'

He took it from her, and she followed him over to the counter and watched him wrap it in tissue paper, then brown paper.

When he finished, his eyes met hers. 'Do you have time for a coffee?'

Georgie checked her watch, then burst out laughing. 'I don't know why I did that. I'm on holidays. I have no plans. Yeah, thanks, Pete, I'd love a coffee.'

He beamed. 'Do you mind watching the gallery for a second? I'll pop over the road to the café. What will you have?'

'Latte is fine. Thanks. Although I probably should be offering to pay for it if you're giving me this.'

'I'll come visit you in Glengarrick some time and you can make me one.'

While he was gone, Georgie wandered around, perusing the other pieces of artwork on display. Pete was exceptionally good. No wonder he'd quit nursing to following his passion. Lucky him. She had it the wrong way around. She'd quit something she was once passionate about to fulfil her obligations.

When Pete returned and handed her the takeaway coffee, they sat on two stools and started chatting easily about a range of topics.

'Will you ever go back to nursing?' Georgie asked.

'Probably not. I loved it, don't get me wrong, but this is where my heart is. Gotta follow your dreams. What about you?' He took a sip of his coffee.

'I wish. But I don't know how I could. I never worked after graduating so I'd probably have to do some sort of refresher course.'

'That's entirely possible. You should investigate. You might be surprised how easy it is to get a job.'

She shrugged. 'Right now, it's not possible. I have a café to run. Besides, I'm not even sure I still want to be a nurse.'

She filled him in about the café and how she'd taken over running it after her mum got sick. Then she told him about her plans for a camp for kids.

'I'm not sure why I'm telling you all this,' she concluded.

'Sometimes it's good to get it all out.'

She nodded.

'I heard about you and Neil.'

She stiffened at the unexpected change of subject even though she wasn't surprised Pete had brought it up. He and Neil had been good mates.

'You probably heard Neil's side of the story. I'm sure it was different from mine.'

'I always thought he didn't deserve you.'

'Thank you.' She wasn't sure what else to say.

Thankfully, Pete sensed she didn't want to talk about Neil, or the past and he moved on, chatting easily about his life which included a wife and new baby. He talked about all sorts of different things with the ease of a man comfortable in his own skin. The time passed quickly, and Georgie was surprised when she glanced at her watch again and saw how late it was. She'd been thoroughly enjoying herself, yet a tiny part of her was jealous too. She envied what Pete had that she didn't.

She stood and put her handbag over her shoulder. 'I should keep going.'

Pete stood too and put a hand on her arm. 'It's been great seeing you again, Georgie.' He hesitated for a second. 'Like I said, you deserve someone much better than Neil. I hope you find him one day.'

Sudden tears sprang to her eyes. 'Thanks, Pete.' She picked up the gift-wrapped photograph. 'You've given me a lot to think about. I'm glad I bumped into you. Make sure if you and your family are ever in Glengarrick you stop in for that coffee.'

When she returned to her car, the tears flowed. For the life of her she couldn't figure out why, except maybe something about Pete reminded her of Jed. A man who had himself together, who knew what he wanted out of life, and was brave enough to make it happen.

***

As Georgie drove towards Glengarrick the following night, the setting sun painted the landscape in brilliant shades of blues, pinks, yellows, and reds. She rounded a bend and came to the top of a small hill which dipped down and followed the edge of the valley back towards home. She slowed down the way she always did at this point on the drive along this road. She'd seen the view countless times at various times of the day, but it never ceased to captivate her as the sun brought out different features over the valley. Her favourite time to enjoy this view was sunset which was why she'd left Beechworth late in the afternoon.

She crested the rise and pulled over to the side of the road.

Even though there had been days when she'd felt trapped living in Glengarrick, she loved it. What she wasn't loving as much anymore was the responsibility of running the café.

When she'd gone home to look after her dad, taking on the café had been a no-brainer when she realised her mum wasn't up to it. It was the right thing to do. Talking with Pete had made her realise how much time she'd lost. It was hard not to look back and be resentful.

But it wasn't just her chat with Pete. Jed coming back home for the weekend had been another catalyst. Jed had been right. Pete was right. Georgie wasn't living *her* dream. She was living her parent's dream.

Neither men would know it, but they'd helped her see she needed to make some big changes. She couldn't keep running the café indefinitely. Not when she'd started to voice her dreams of the camp for kids. The ideal scenario would be Mum getting well enough to run the café again, but that wasn't looking likely. Georgie rested her chin on her hands on the steering wheel. Regardless of what happened with Mum or with the café, she had to find a way to move forward with her life, whether Jed was part of that or not.

After listening to Pete share about his wife, it had brought Georgie's loneliness to the fore. None of her school friendship group were married yet, but they all had significant others, even Zara. Everyone except her.

And Jed. Unless he and Annabel Norton were an item.

She exhaled slowly. When had life gotten so difficult? Or had it always been this way and she was having some weird sort of awakening?

She couldn't stop thinking about what she wanted. Someone to share life with. She wanted someone to snuggle up in bed with on a Saturday morning or playfully bicker over the control of the TV remote. She wanted holidays and someone to make family traditions with. She wanted someone to give her a nickname. And, one day, she wanted children.

A cloud passed overhead, briefly blocking out the sun and causing shadows to dance across the valley. A car slowed almost to a stop as it drove by and the driver, a P-plater, looked at her, eyebrows raised as he pointed to her car. She gave him a wave and a thumbs up to show she was okay. He nodded and drove off. She turned off the ignition and got out of the car, welcoming the silence. Resting back against the warm hood of the car, she gazed up at the sky and at the first stars shining back at her. When she was a kid, her dad said God tossed out crushed diamonds every night and waited for them to land on a sky made of velvet.

Tonight, as the light faded and darkness closed in, Georgie did something she hadn't done in years. She made a wish.

Chapter 20

The first test was positive.

To be certain, Georgie drove into Stockton after work, bought a pack of three pregnancy kits from a different chemist, and did the test twice more that night before bundling the little sticks together, wrapping them in a tissue and throwing them in the bin.

Two blue lines. The condom must have broken without either of them realising it.

A spark of joy ignited, followed immediately by a breath of fear. What was Jed going to say?

Georgie's heartbeat whooshed through her ears. Slumping back against the bathroom bench, she closed her eyes, stared heavenward and offered a silent prayer for help. When no booming voice from above answered, she gave herself a mental shake and swallowed the desire to cry. It wasn't just Jed she had to worry about telling. How was she going to tell Mum? Her friends? She could hardly hide a growing bump from the eyes of the women in Glengarrick either.

After showering, Georgie stood and stared at her body in the full-length mirror. She hadn't recognised the early symptoms for what they were because she'd put her malaise down to emotional exhaustion. She'd been off her food too but had put that down to fatigue rather than recognising the slight nausea for what it was. Morning sickness. She did a rough calculation and figured she was about seven weeks pregnant. No wonder she'd been bone tired and her breasts ached.

Georgie got into bed and stared up at the ceiling. For a split second, she allowed herself to picture life with Jed beside her and a baby in a bassinet at the end of the bed, but the dream instantly shattered. Evidently that night hadn't meant anything to him. Her mouth dried. How would he feel if he knew their lovemaking had resulted in a baby?

She put a protective hand on her flat stomach as doubts and questions pinged around her head. What would she do if she told Jed and he didn't want to be part of her—or the baby's—life? She exhaled slowly. If only they hadn't slept together. But she couldn't turn back the clock. As Dad would have said: "too late to close the gates, love. The horse has already bolted".

She'd call Jed tomorrow and whatever he said, she'd deal with it. The same way she dealt with all the blows that came her way.

With stoicism.

*****

It was three weeks before Georgie finally went to Stockton to see a GP who confirmed she was ten-weeks pregnant. She still hadn't found the courage to call Jed. She tried to convince herself she was too busy at work, but really, she was too scared to tell him for fear of his reaction. It wasn't the kind of conversation she wanted to have on the phone either. She contemplated driving to Melbourne and showing up at his place, but she didn't even know where he lived, and she didn't want to text him in case he didn't reply.

On Friday night, instead of being at home with her feet up watching Netflix, she was camped out in the kitchen at the café, doing her best to prepare food for the weekend. She was one staff member down after her chef, Reece, had an altercation with a chainsaw. He'd been cutting down a tree and sliced off the end of his finger. It had required microsurgery. Gutted to let her down, he'd made a few phone calls from hospital and arranged for a mate of his from Melbourne to come to Glengarrick to help out. Unfortunately, Brett couldn't get there until Tuesday, which left Georgie two options. She could close the café for the weekend and lose money. Or she could do her best to cover the kitchen and hope Brett was as good as Reece said he was and leave it in his capable hands on Tuesday morning.

She didn't want to close. The café was busy and doing well and shutting the doors would put a dent in her budget. In the early days after she took over from Mum there were times when she thought she'd have to close, but she'd persevered. Now the café was humming and making a profit. Not a lot, but enough that she was putting money into her savings account every week. She almost had enough for a deposit on a house.

She'd never given much thought to having a baby, but she hadn't imagined pregnancy would be like this. She wanted to celebrate and to enjoy the changes taking place in her body, but she didn't want to do it alone. Not being able to share her news with anyone was difficult, but until she'd told Jed, she couldn't tell anyone else, not even Zara.

Closing her eyes, Georgie took a deep cleansing breath, hoping to settle the flurry of butterflies in her stomach. She had to stop finding excuses not to call Jed and tell him. Nursing the secret was giving her heartburn. Or perhaps that was the pregnancy.

A fresh batch of tears came from nowhere. She'd been doing fine until Jed walked back into her life and tossed everything in the air as easily as he flung a football around.

'Why did I sleep with him?' she muttered as she went back to cutting pumpkin into cubes ready to make a batch of soup. Even the music she had pumping through the sound system wasn't lifting her mood. She switched it off, plunging the kitchen into silence. Who needed late night love songs, anyway?

A noise out the side caught her attention and she stopped what she was doing. Straining, she listened harder, expecting to hear the scratching of a possum running across the roof. Hopefully it wasn't a rat in the walls again. That was the last thing she needed in the kitchen right now.

The noise came again, and her stomach lurched. This time she heard the unmistakable sound of footsteps on gravel. Whoever it was, they weren't making any effort to be quiet.

Striding over to the wall, she flipped the outside lights on hoping to scare off whoever was out there.

Glengarrick didn't have a crime problem so it was probably someone who'd had a few too many drinks and they'd got confused and thought the café was their home. Or perhaps it was kids fooling around. Heaven knew she and her friends used to get up to mischief some Friday nights. Glengarrick didn't have a drug problem either, but the back of the café would make a great place for kids to hide and have a smoke or inject drugs without being seen.

Seconds later, a tap on the front window made her jump and her already racing pulse went into double time.

'Georgie? It's Jed.'

She gasped then exhaled in a rush. With a shaking hand, she opened the front door. Jed stood there with a sheepish look on his face.

'What are you trying to do? Give me a heart attack?' she asked.

'Sorry. I tried knocking but I don't think you heard me over the music. So, I went down the side to knock on the back door, then the lights came on. I didn't mean to frighten you.'

'You're lucky I didn't call the police.'

'I'm really sorry.'

She held the door open wider and took a step back. 'Are you coming in?'

'Is that okay?'

She nodded.

'What are you doing here so late?' he asked as he followed her into the kitchen.

She gestured to the stainless-steel benches covered in food. 'What does it look like?'

'Making a mess?'

She let out a shaky breath. 'For what it's worth, you caught me having a pity party.'

He frowned.

She explained what had happened to Reece and why she was cooking, blaming that for her funk. Telling Jed the truth would have to wait. She couldn't spring it on him now. Not until she knew why he was here.

She glanced up at the clock on the wall. It was after ten. 'What are *you* doing here so late?' she asked. A text to let her know he was coming back might have been nice. 'Is everything okay?'

His shoulders dropped.

'By that look, should I offer you a drink?'

'Probably not. I stopped at the pub first. I've already had a couple of beers.'

She pushed aside the food she was preparing. 'This can wait. Grab a seat.'

Jed took a stool down from the bench and sat while Georgie went to the fridge and pulled out two Sprites.

'You hungry?' she asked, putting a drink in front of him.

'Is that a trick question? I'm always hungry.'

Glad for something to do so she had a minute to think, Georgie went back to the fridge, pulled out an assortment of finger food and placed it in the microwave. While she waited for it to heat, she concentrated on slowing her breathing. She couldn't believe Jed was acting as though it was totally normal for him to be sitting at her bench like he belonged there. Meanwhile, her insides were doing somersaults.

'Thanks, George, this looks great,' he said when she put the food in front of him.

She pulled down a stool and sat next to him, waiting for him to eat and take a sip of his drink before she spoke. 'So, what's going on? Is everything okay?'

'I've decided not to stay in Melbourne.'

She raised her eyebrows but said nothing.

'It wasn't working.'

'You quit?' she asked softly. Jed wasn't the type who gave up easily, so things must have been bad.

He shook his head. 'I was on a three-month probation period. They understood when I said I couldn't continue.'

'Why?'

He shrugged. 'I remember hearing that a lot of former players struggle after they give the game away, but I didn't think I'd be one of them. You know, they talk about not being able to find anything to fill the void. Not being able to find a job or work they enjoy. That's why I figured a job at a club would be the best option. But watching the boys run out and knowing I couldn't join them. It was too hard.'

Georgie put her hand on his arm and squeezed. She had no words that would take away the pain she heard in his voice.

'When the doctors told me I needed to retire, it hit me like a ton of bricks. I thought I was invincible.'

'Surely you didn't think you could play forever.'

'I thought I had at least another five years in me. I was still in great form and playing well, then bang, I was done in one week. It was like a massive hole opened right in front of me. I felt like I'd lost my family. Every day I used to go to work with forty of my best mates. Everything we did was for a common goal. We trained, played, and socialised together. Then it was gone. The moment I finished playing it all ground to a halt. The coaches tell you about it, but I wasn't prepared.'

'Is it the camaraderie you miss, or do you miss playing too?'

'Playing. I can't begin to explain how much I miss it. Unless you've done it, it's hard to describe what it's like to run out onto the MCG in front of fifty thousand people.' His eyes bore into hers. 'What nine-to-five job is going to give me that sort of buzz?'

'Is that what you miss most? The buzz?' There was more to life than working for a "buzz", but she didn't say that.

He inhaled and exhaled. 'It's a hard feeling to describe. I figured if I was assistant coaching, I'd be on the ground on game day and feel part of it, but it was the opposite. There was this huge chasm between me and the players.'

'I'm really not sure what to say, Jed, or what to suggest you do.'

'No-one does. I mean, how many men approaching thirty have never had a normal job?' He glanced down at his empty plate. 'What am I supposed to do with the rest of my life?'

'I think that's a question we all ask ourselves at some point.'

He sighed again. 'I know. And I should be grateful. If I spoke like this to anyone else, I know what they'd say. "Get over yourself". And they'd be right. I mean, why should they feel sorry for me? I should be counting my blessings because for ten years I've lived the dream and earned good money.'

'Money isn't everything.'

'No, it's not.'

'So, if you have enough money, why can't you take time off and sit and think about the future? I mean, what's the rush?'

'You're right. There's no rush, which is why I'm home.'

A tiny needle of disappointment pricked her. He hadn't come back to see her. He'd only come home because he had nowhere else to go. She stood and started clearing away his plate and their empty drinks.

Jed put a hand on hers to stop her. 'I came back to see you too, George.'

She froze. 'What…what do you mean?'

'We didn't…*I* didn't leave well. After that night I…I shouldn't have walked out on you without giving a relationship with you a chance. I shouldn't have taken a job over us.'

Georgie's breathing quickened. She met his gaze and swallowed before speaking. 'Us?' Her voice quivered.

He reached for her hands and gave her a small smile and Georgie's heart went from a trot to a gallop.

'I don't know what I want to do in terms of a job and that's okay. Like you said, there's no rush. But as for us?' He searched her eyes. 'I'm hoping you'll tell me what you'd like to do.'

She pictured handing him a tiny baby, and her heart stuttered. 'Do you have plans tomorrow night?'

'I don't have any plans, full stop.'

'How about we have that dinner you promised?' That would give her the right opportunity to break her news. Then he could decide if there was still an "us" to talk about. 'I'll cook.'

A slow grin spread over his face. 'I'd love that. I'd love that a lot.'

Chapter 21

It had rained lightly on and off all day, but by six o'clock, the clouds had darkened, and it had turned into a steady drizzle. Georgie paused at the window of the café and looked out. Jed's car was parked out the front, but there was no sign of him. She rubbed her arms. Where was he?

She'd tossed and turned all night and today she'd come up with a dozen different ways to tell him she was pregnant, but none of them felt right. She'd even Googled "how to announce a surprise pregnancy" in the hope it would help. It hadn't. The internet was full of ideas for how to break the news including "world's best parent" T-shirts, romantic dinners that ended with pastel-coloured cupcakes, or dogs carrying handwritten notes. The funniest one she'd seen was a woman who had written the message on her soon-to-be-bulging belly. She'd rolled her eyes at that.

A flash of movement caught her eye and she spotted Jed coming out of the local IGA. He carried a brown paper bag in one hand, a bouquet of flowers in his other and a green shopping bag hung over the crook of his arm.

When she'd messaged him earlier that morning to make sure he was still okay for dinner, she'd warned him she was sick of cooking. All she had to offer was soup and freshly baked sourdough bread. He'd replied with a smiling emoji and said he was coming for the company, not the food.

A flush of warmth had shot through her when she'd read that message, but now the warmth was replaced by uncertainty. She had no idea how he'd take the news.

As she watched him stroll back to the café, the skies opened, and the fine drizzle turned into a deluge. He started to jog.

She opened the front door and beckoned to him. 'Jed! Run!'

He hesitated for a moment then thunder rumbled, and he bolted down the footpath, changing direction and crossing the road, veering towards her, head down, clutching the flowers to his chest like they were a football and he was heading towards an open goal. He sprinted up the steps and burst inside the café as the entire sky was lit by a crack of lightning followed instantly by the boom of thunder.

Georgie closed the door behind him.

'Where did that come from?' he asked.

He was dripping wet and his hair was plastered to his head as water ran in rivulets down his cheeks. When he shook his head, she stepped back. He reminded her of a wet Golden Retriever.

'You're soaked!' she exclaimed. 'Let me take these and grab

you some towels.' With shaking hands, she took the flowers, the bag of groceries and bottle of wine from him and put them on the counter while he shrugged out of his wet jacket and slung it over the back of a chair.

She'd braced herself for some kind of awkwardness between them, and even though her heart was racing, and her insides were twisting in knots, Jed appeared to be as relaxed as always.

When she returned with a stack of tea towels, she found him in the kitchen near the stove, with a spoon in hand ready to dip it into the saucepan.

He shot her a guilty look. 'Sorry, I'm starving.'

She tossed him the towels and batted him away from the stove with a wooden spoon. 'Dry off first then I'll serve you some soup.'

He scrubbed at his wet hair with the towel. 'Hope you don't mind that I bought a few things from the IGA.' He pointed to the shopping bag she'd put on the counter.

'Not at all.' She pulled out two types of cheese, three different paper wrapped bags of deli meat, a jar of sundried tomatoes, two dips, a box of crackers and a jar of dukkha. There was enough food for a small party. 'Are you expecting a crowd, or didn't you think my soup would be enough?'

He had the grace to look embarrassed. 'To be honest, I eat a lot and I wasn't sure soup alone would fill me up.'

'You haven't tried my soup yet,' she said, 'or my bread. But thanks, this will go well with it.'

He might be hungry, but food was the last thing on Georgie's mind. While he finished towelling himself off, she pulled out a timber board and put together all the ingredients into a charcuterie platter. She hoped he wasn't watching too closely because her hands wouldn't stop shaking.

As she pushed the platter towards him, he flashed her a huge smile. 'Wow, that looks incredible. Good enough to eat.'

'Over the years I've picked up a few tips from Reece. Let's go and sit over there.'

She pointed to a table she'd set for them in a corner. She hadn't wanted to go overboard, but she'd lit a few candles and dotted them around the café where they provided shimmering light and decadent scents. She'd also drawn all the blinds so anyone walking past couldn't look in and see them. Hopefully Jed wouldn't think she was trying to force intimacy on them. It wasn't supposed to be a date, just a chance to catch up and talk in private.

And for you to tell him your news, a little voice in her head reminded her.

Jed took the platter over to the table and as she carried two bowls of steaming soup over to him, lightning flashed again followed a split second later by a rumble of thunder. The lights went out, flickered back on, then went off, plunging the café into near darkness.

'Lucky I lit the candles,' she said with a shaky laugh.

'I don't care about the power. I'm only glad you heated the

soup before it went off.' Jed eyed his bowl like a man who hadn't eaten in a week. He leaned in close and inhaled deeply. 'What kind is it?'

'Um, potato and leek.'

Jed started to eat, while she swirled the soup with her spoon.

'Not hungry?' he asked, glancing up after a few mouthfuls.

'Not really. I've been snacking all day.' It wasn't a lie. Snacking kept her nausea at bay and today she'd been more queasy than normal as worry had knotted itself in the bottom of her gut.

The rain was pounding so loudly on the roof they had to raise their voices to be heard. Her anxiety notched up. Shouting her announcement wasn't what she had in mind.

By the time Jed had finished eating, the storm had passed, and the rain had eased. She cleared her throat. It was time to tell him. She couldn't keep pretending this was simply two friends catching up for a casual dinner. Yesterday he'd said he'd come home for her and he wanted to talk about them and their relationship. First, she needed to see if her news would send him away.

She opened her mouth to speak when Jed shot to his feet. 'Let's go for a drive.'

Georgie blinked and stared up at him. 'What? Now? Where?' she stammered. 'It's pitch black. Anyway, I thought the whole idea of dinner was so we could talk.'

'Who said we can't talk while we drive?' Jed flashed a smile. 'Besides, I have a surprise for you.'

She sucked in a breath. 'Surprise?' She hated surprises.

He took he hand. 'I promise you'll love it.'

As she grabbed her jacket, she blew out a long slow breath. Maybe Jed was just as nervous as she was. Whatever happened, she'd tell him tonight, no matter what.

After blowing out all the candles and locking up the café, they headed outside.

'Where are we going?' she asked.

Glengarrick on a Saturday night wasn't exactly a ghost town, but it wasn't like there were lots of options for places to go. The only places open were the fish and chip shop, the Indian restaurant or the Chinese takeaway and they'd already eaten so they didn't need to go there. There was always the pub. But they definitely weren't going *there*. That would set tongues wagging.

Jed pointed his key fob at his car. 'You'll see.'

***

They drove down the main street before turning onto the highway, heading towards Stockton. Georgie frowned. Stockton was a much bigger town than Glengarrick, but she couldn't think why he wanted to drive there at this time of night.

She jiggled her knee.

'You cold?' he asked.

'A little.'

He turned up the heat, then pressed a button on the screen on the dash. Lady Gaga's voice filled the car.

She glanced over at him. It was hard to see his face in the dark. 'Really? Lady Gaga. Wouldn't have thought this would be your musical taste.'

He chuckled. 'I don't think she is, but a friend told me I needed to watch a movie she was in and since then I've been listening to the soundtrack.' He shrugged. 'This is just a Spotify playlist. Can't say I'm a fan of her music but I loved her in that movie.'

'*A Star is Born.*'

He nodded and glanced sideways at her. 'Have you seen it.'

'Lost count of how many times I've watched it.' She tried to see in his face in the dark. 'Did you like it?'

'Loved it.'

For the rest of the drive Jed kept up a one-sided conversation, chatting easily about his favourite movies and music and what books he liked reading. She noted that he avoided anything too deep or personal, but she couldn't blame him for that. She wasn't giving him much more than one-word answers.

Twenty minutes later Jed pulled off the main highway and his headlights picked up a simple sign: Stockton Outdoor Cinema. Georgie frowned. Watching a movie ruled out any chance of talking properly. She glanced across at Jed again. Was this his way of avoiding a serious conversation? Her head pounded, and she had to force herself to slow her breathing. This wasn't how she'd planned the night, but it would be rude to tell Jed to turn around and go home.

'Have you ever been here?' he asked as he turned in the driveway.

She shook her head. 'I never even knew this place existed.'

'Apparently it's an institution. I've never been either, and I'm not sure what's playing tonight, but when I heard about it, I thought we should go. It's only open once a month. Don't hold it against me if it's nothing but a Disney princess movie.'

She tried to laugh but it sounded forced. She sighed inwardly. All she had to do was watch the movie, then she'd tell him.

Jed paid the entrance fee to the teenager manning the booth at the front gate, then drove slowly into the paddock that doubled as the drive-in parking space. There was a screen set up at the far end and a few rows of cars already parked in place. He picked a spot at the end of the back row and pulled in.

'Do you want some popcorn?' he asked after turning off the engine.

She shook her head. How could he still be hungry? 'I'm not hungry, but I'd love a drink, please. Just water.'

Georgie watched him head across to the food vans set up near the front gate. Another car pulled into the spot next to theirs, and she turned and saw the green and white P-plates in the windscreen and two teenagers. The boy shut off his engine, then promptly reached over and started kissing the girl in the passenger seat. Georgie averted her gaze. This was a mistake. They should have stayed at the café and talked.

She turned her gaze back to the food vans and watched Jed weave his way back to the car. When he got back, she reached over to open the door for him. His arms were laden with snacks. As well as the oversized bucket of popcorn, he had two Magnum ice creams, a bag of lollies and two bottles of water.

'Overboard, much?' she asked.

'Maybe I went a little wild,' he agreed.

'A little?' she echoed.

He glanced over her shoulder at the other car and threw back his head and laughed. 'Do you think they'll remember what movie they watched?'

'Ah. No.'

He took a handful of popcorn and put it in his mouth. Cringeworthy local ads played on the screen but she barely noticed. Jed was too near and this was all too weird.

'Do we know what we're watching?' she asked.

'Mm hm.' He swallowed. 'Would you believe *Grease*?'

She smiled. 'Why am I not surprised?'

'Hope our neighbours don't mind if we sing along.' He reached for the radio and tuned it to right station, then pushed his seat back like he didn't have a care in the world.

The opening soundtrack started, and the movie appeared on

the screen. As much as she tried, Georgie couldn't focus on the movie. Even though she knew every word to every song and could have easily sung along, she was jittery and fidgety, like she'd drunk too much coffee.

Halfway through the movie, Jed turned down the volume and put his hand on her arm. 'You okay?'

'Sure. Yeah. I'm fine.' She smiled, reached over for a handful of popcorn, and shoved it in her mouth.

Why wouldn't I be fine?

Chapter 22

Jed barely watched any of the movie. A button on Georgie's shirt had worked its way undone, giving him a teasing glimpse of the soft white skin of her breast. He had to force himself not to keep staring at her.

If he'd had any doubts about his feelings for Georgie, they vanished as soon as he'd seen her tonight. He made a mental note to thank Annabel for giving him the kick up the butt he'd needed to come back and address things with Georgie.

All night, memories of the night they'd made love flooded his brain: the sure, confident heat of Georgie's mouth and the feel of her body pressed against his. He was tied up in knots trying to pretend he was cool and calm when he was anything but. His spur of the moment decision to go to the drive-in movie was to buy time. He wasn't normally so unsure of himself but talking about his feelings for her had him scrambling for more time. He thought the movie would be a good idea but being in the car with her was excruciating. She was so close to him he could almost taste her. It made him kind of jealous of the kids in the car next to them. He'd wanted the timing to be perfect before he asked Georgie if she'd consider a future with him. Now, he felt like he'd ruined everything. They should have stayed at the café. With the candles and soft music it had been intimate and perfect.

He snuck another look at Georgie's face, illuminated in the taillights of the cars in front of his. He breathed in and out slowly and tried to slow his racing heart. He didn't want to scare her off, but he had to tell her his feelings ran deep. Problem was, he wanted to do that face to face, not in the darkness of his car. He clenched and unclenched his hands around the steering wheel. It was so frustrating that he couldn't even suggest they go back to his place. Or hers. If he moved back to Glengarrick and she agreed to go out with him, the first thing he needed to do was find a place of his own.

Georgie was the first to break the silence. 'Do want to go back to the café? I can make you a coffee.'

He let out a breath of relief. She'd read his mind. 'Great idea.'

They drove in thick silence. After five minutes, he couldn't stand it for another moment. Flicking on the indicator, he pulled off the road and parked. He left the car running and the heater on. After removing his seat belt, he twisted in his seat and faced her.

'I've stuffed this all up.'

He flicked on the internal light and she blinked. 'Stuffed what up?'

'Everything. Coming home without telling you I was coming. Going to a drive in instead of sitting down and talking.' He exhaled softly. 'Three months ago, I made a dumb decision when I took that job. Thank goodness a friend told me I was a fool.'

She licked her lips but didn't say anything. She wasn't making it easy, but he probably deserved her hesitation.

Heart hammering, he reached for her hands and entwined his fingers with hers. 'My friend told me if I had such a soft spot for a certain woman in Glengarrick, I needed to go home and tell her.'

'A soft spot?' Georgie's echoed question was barely more than a whisper.

He stroked her cheek. 'More than a soft spot. I was actually in love with this woman ten years ago, but I didn't realise it until recently. I've been a fool for taking so long to figure it out.'

Georgie's chest rose and fell with each breath.

'Something incredible happened a few months back but I did something dumb. I put my career before her. That's why I needed to get home and find out if things between me and this woman were as good as I remembered. To see if the woman I'm crazy about might be crazy about me.'

Her eyes widened, but she still didn't say anything.

'I need to know, Georgie, did I get it wrong? Do you have feelings for me?'

'You didn't get it wrong,' she whispered.

'I'm glad,' he whispered back.

He leaned across the centre console and when their lips met, memories rekindled, quickly fanning them into flames. Her fingers crept into his hair and he closed his eyes and inhaled her perfume.

Seconds later, his body went into a shuddering free fall. He didn't care that they were no different from the kids in the car next to them at the drive-in cinema. All he cared was getting closer to Georgie and feeling her skin on his fingertips. He pulled her closer, tracing a finger from her lips to her chin, down the hollow of her throat to the swell of her breast.

She pulled back suddenly and gasped. 'Don't.'

The word was so at odds with how she was responding to him that for a split-second Jed thought he was hearing things. But her hands pushed him away and her eyes dropped to her lap, avoiding his gaze.

'This isn't right,' she murmured.

'Feels right to me,' he replied, although he would have preferred to be somewhere private and comfortable—preferably a bed—not on the side of the road in his car.

'Is that why you came back?' she asked. 'For sex?'

He jerked back at the pain in her tone. 'No!' He gently turned her chin and made her look at him. 'Is that what you think?'

'Well, both times we've made love, you've left. What am I supposed to think?' She fiddled with the button on her shirt. 'How do I know you won't leave me again?'

He pressed his head to hers. 'I promise I won't.'

He'd failed her twice and wouldn't let it happen again. There was no way he was ever letting this woman out of his sights again. He was going to make the rest of her life the best she'd ever known, because she deserved it.

Her bottom lip wobbled. 'How can I be sure?'

'I'll spend the rest of my life proving it to you. But you'll have to trust me.'

She opened her mouth to say something, then closed it again.

'And as for my joke about the sex…' He hesitated, not wanting his words to come across as crude or crass, but he needed her to know the truth. 'If casual sex was what I wanted, I wouldn't have driven four hours back to Glengarrick for it.'

Her eyebrows rose sharply and the flush on her face deepened.

He sighed. 'I want to give us a go, Georgie. That's why I'm home. To see if we can take this—whatever *this* is—further. There's a spark between us and I know it's worth pursuing. I hope you do, too. We can take things slowly if you want or I can walk away. It's up to you. But you have my word that this time if you say yes, I'm not going anywhere. I want to be with you.'

She shifted in her seat and wouldn't look at him. 'You might not stay when you hear what I have to tell you,' she murmured. Her back was almost against the passenger side door.

His heart dropped into his stomach. What could she possibly say that would make him want to leave again? Surely she hadn't met someone else in the last three months.

'Do you realise where we are?' she asked, pointing out the window.

He looked around. Until then, he hadn't. 'The bridge,' he said softly.

The scene of the accident.

'I shouldn't have kissed you that night,' she said, 'but after the storm, when you held me and promised you'd make sure no-one knew the truth of what happened, I trusted you.'

He took her hands again. 'And I took advantage of that trust by sleeping with you.'

She shook her head. 'No. That night we both wanted it.'

He remembered. Her kisses had been tentative at first, but there was no doubt she'd given herself willingly to their lovemaking. As had he. Guided by her touch, fuelled by his desire for her and the fact neither of them had slept with anyone else, they'd bonded in a way he hadn't thought possible.

'I'm sorry,' she said finally letting out a ragged sigh. 'It's not you, it's me.'

He waited for her to elaborate, sensing she was wrestling with something massive.

'I'm pregnant.'

The world stopped for a second and Jed's mouth went as dry as sand. The only sound in the car was the pounding in his temples.

'Mine?' he whispered, wishing he didn't have to ask.

She dragged her eyes to meet his and slowly nodded.

He swore softly as he reached for her hands. He searched her face. 'Are you okay? How are you feeling? When did you find out?'

'I'm good. Really good.' She gave him a half smile.

'How far along are you?'

'Twelve weeks.'

He stared into the glassy pools of her eyes. 'Were you going to tell me?'

She nodded. 'Yes, of course. I've been trying to tell you all night.'

He released her hands, sat back in the seat, and stared out at the darkness around them letting the enormity of her news wash over him. No wonder she'd been acting so strangely all night.

'I'm sorry, Jed.'

He turned to her. 'Why are you sorry?'

'I didn't plan for this.'

'It's okay. Sometimes the best things are the things we don't plan for.'

He wanted to believe his own words, but self-doubt and uncertainty rushed in. He ran his hands through his hair and exhaled loudly.

'This is going to take some getting used to. I've never thought about having kids.'

'You don't have to—'

He cut her off. 'I want to. It's just I have no idea how to be a good dad.' His own father hadn't been much use to him as a role model.

'And you think I know how to be a good mother?'

'For what it's worth, I know you'll make a wonderful mum.'

She blinked back tears. 'Thank you, Jed. That means a lot.'

He tucked a strand of hair behind her ear. 'I don't suppose anyone knows how to be a good parent before they have a baby. I guess we'll have to figure it out together.'

'I love you, Jed.'

'I love you, too.'

'You said something earlier.' She tilted her head. 'That you've loved me for a long time but only just realised it.'

He nodded.

'Even before you rescued me that night,' she said, with fresh tears in her eyes, 'I loved you.'

He somehow managed to hold it together as he leaned over and awkwardly held her. She was trembling and he wished they were somewhere other than his car so he could hold her properly and tell her everything was going to be alright.

With Georgie leaning against his chest, he felt the thumping of her heart and he tightened his arms around her. As he kissed the top of her head, he couldn't stop the smile from forming. They were having a baby! He was going to be a father. He tenderly stroked Georgie's cheek. He was never letting her, or their baby, go.

When they kissed, it was sweet and deep and trembling at first, but it was full of passion and the promise of what was to come.

Chapter 23

The next six weeks were a blur for Georgie. Jed resigned from his job with the Bombers, pulled out of the lease of his apartment at Docklands, put his house in Geelong on the market and rented a small house for them in Glengarrick. She took two weeks off work and moved in. They spent every moment together setting up their home and catching up on all the time it felt like they'd missed out on.

When everyone found out they were a couple they were thrilled. When they also told people Georgie was pregnant, they'd been inundated with housewarming gifts and presents for the baby.

The best thing was how excited their mothers were. Jed's mum reached out to Jane and they'd caught up for a coffee a couple of times.

When Georgie had Facetimed Zara to tell her the news, her friend's reaction was a classic.

'Shut the front gate. You are *not!* How? When did this happen?'

Georgie laughed. 'The weekend of the Grand Final.'

'I cannot believe you didn't say anything.'

'When have I been one to gossip?'

'For your information, it's not gossiping if you're telling your best friend. How far along are you?'

'Nearly eighteen weeks. We have the ultrasound next week.'

'How are you feeling?'

'Not as exhausted now.'

'That's good. My sisters said the second trimester is the best. Just so you know, I want to be the godmother.'

Georgie grinned. 'As if we'd chose anyone else.'

'How did your mum take the news?'

'Really well. I think this is just what she needed. Last time I popped home to pick something up, Michelle was there teaching Mum to knit.'

'Was Jed shocked when you told him?'

'Yep. As shocked as me. But he's thrilled,' she added quickly.

'Don't take this the wrong way George, but do you think you two would have gotten together if you weren't pregnant?'

Georgie nodded. 'Yeah. He came back to ask me out. That's when I told him I was pregnant.'

Zara sat back in her chair. 'I'm so happy for you.'

'How are things with you and Kath?'

Zara screwed up her nose. 'Let's just say I don't think she'd be as thrilled as Jed if I told her I was pregnant.'

Georgie stared at her friend. 'Are you?'

Zara shook her head. 'No. But I've started to think I wouldn't mind having kids one day.' She smiled. 'For now, I'm happy to help you look after yours.' She glanced at something off the screen. 'Hey, listen, I gotta go. But call me after the ultrasound. I want to know the sex of this kid so I can start buying it stuff.'

Georgie had chuckled as they'd disconnected the call. She couldn't remember a time she'd felt so happy.

***

A week later Georgie lay on the narrow examination table in the darkened radiography room at the hospital in Stockton. Her T-shirt was hoisted up around her armpits and her jeans were unzipped and lowered over her hips.

Georgie hated that they'd started without Jed, but he'd called to say he'd be late. He'd gotten stuck behind a herd of cows being shifted from one paddock to another.

Not long after starting the scan, Amira, the radiographer, left the cubicle, mumbling something about needing to chat to someone.

Georgie ran a hand over the tiny bulge—the baby was about the size of a capsicum—and wondered if what she could feel was actually her bursting bladder, not the baby. She smiled. Other than being chronically tired, she'd had a dream pregnancy, with only a bit of nausea early on.

But today something felt different and she couldn't put her finger on what it was. Maybe it was just because Jed wasn't here yet. She dragged in a deep breath and exhaled slowly, forcing herself to relax. He'd be here soon.

Georgie liked to have all contingencies planned for and didn't like surprises, so today was her second ultrasound, but the first one Jed was able to get to. She'd had an earlier one to confirm her dates, and he'd been stuck in Melbourne and couldn't make it. She didn't want him to miss this one too.

They wanted to find out the sex of the baby so they could paint the walls of the nursery and buy baby clothes. Georgie harboured a secret hope for a little girl to dress in pink and take to ballet lessons. Jed was positive they were having a boy who would grow up riding horses and chasing footballs like he had. Either way, as cliché as it sounded, neither of them cared about the sex of their baby, as long as he or she was healthy.

Georgie tenderly rubbed her belly again. She'd only recently felt the tiny beating of her baby's feet like butterfly wings.

While she waited for Amira to return, she sent Jed another text message.

How far away are you?

Just parked the car. I'll be there in five.

She was sending him a reply when Amira re-entered with another woman. When she cleared her throat, Georgie jumped and tucked her phone in her back pocket. 'Sorry. I was texting Jed. He'll be here soon.'

'Georgina, this is Corrine. She's the senior radiologist. I've asked her to have a look at your scan.'

Something in Amira's tone caused a ripple of unease to trickle down Georgie's spine. 'Sure.'

She pulled up her top again.

Corrine scooted closer to Georgie on her saddle stool and plucked the ultrasound wand from its clip on the side of the machine. Covering it in gel, she angled the screen away enough that Georgie couldn't see it. Outside was the muted sound of traffic, but inside the room was quiet, except for the faint whoosh of air through the vents.

Corrine lifted the ultrasound wand in the air before laying it on Georgie's abdomen. 'Sorry it's going to be cold.' She pressed firmly, moving the wand from side to side.

Georgie closed her eyes, held her breath and waited for the galloping lub-dub sound she'd heard last time.

Nothing.

Corrine manoeuvred the wand to the other side and pressed harder. Still nothing. When she didn't say anything, the tiny trickle of disquiet going through Georgie became a raging torrent of fear.

'Is your husband far away?' Corrine asked kindly.

'My partner,' Georgie corrected her, although it made no difference what she called Jed. Husband. Partner. Boyfriend. They were a couple. 'He should be here any moment. He probably stopped to pick up a coffee.'

Corrine lowered the wand to Georgie's belly again. Thick, ugly, deafening silence descended on the room. Corrine angled the screen towards Georgie. Staring at it, dread flooded her veins. It didn't take an expert to see there was no movement. No fluttering heartbeat like last time. No arms waving. No legs kicking. No thumb sucking. The image on the screen might as well have been a screen shot, not a live view. For a moment Georgie told herself that's what it was. A still image. But when neither Corrine nor Amira said anything, fear gripped her insides like an icy vice, and she knew.

She knew.

A buzzing sounded in her ears and her vision blurred as the room spun. She dragged in a deep breath, gripped the examination table with both hands and willed herself not to pass out. Lying as still as she could she breathed slowly in and out through her nose, silently begging the tiny baby to move.

Time stopped, and she only shifted position when she became aware of how stiff her neck was from staring incredulously at the frozen white image on the black screen. She blinked as tears burned behind her eyelids.

Please let me wake up from this nightmare, she begged.

A hush fell over the room.

Say something. She stared mutely at the women. *Just say it.*

Tell me. Tell me the truth. My baby is dead, isn't he? It had been clear looking at the image that the baby was a boy.

Someone was crying and it was only when Corrine squeezed her arm, Georgie realised the sound was coming from her.

Amira helped Georgie into a sitting position.

'I'm dreadfully sorry, Georgina.' Corrine paused as if choosing her words carefully. 'As you can see, there's no heartbeat.' Her eyes were full of sympathy and her words were soft and filled with compassion, yet they hit Georgie harder than a punch to the gut.

With those two simple words, all the elation, the excitement, the anticipation she'd felt, totally vanished. Their baby had no heartbeat.

She tried to swallow, tried to speak, tried to breathe, tried to process what Corrine was saying—something about needing to get the baby out—but she couldn't concentrate. This wasn't happening. *Couldn't* be happening.

Moments later Georgie heard Jed's voice in the hallway and fresh tears filled her eyes. He would be as gutted as she was. There was a hesitant knock, then Jed stepped into the room, singing out his apologies for being late, a tray of takeaway coffees held high.

A sob ripped from deep inside taking with it all the air from her lungs.

Tears trickled down her cheeks, unchecked. As much as they hadn't planned to have a baby, miscarriage wasn't part of their pregnancy game plan.

Jed skidded to a stop. As he placed the coffees on the bench, the colour drained from his face and his smile slipped and fell. 'What's wrong? What's going on?' He glanced from Georgie to the Amira and Corrine and back.

'I'm so sorry,' Corrine said softly. 'There's no heartbeat.'

Hearing the words again, an invisible vice tightened around Georgie's heart and a clammy sensation crept over her skin. Time ground to a halt. Jed looked around as if wondering if he'd walked into the wrong room. Pain twisted his face into a grimace before he rushed to her side and pulled her into his arms. They clung to each other while she cried.

'There must be a mistake,' he said finally, looking up.

Corrine shook her head. 'I'm sorry. There's no mistake.' She switched off the ultrasound machine and the faint whirring stopped, then the screen went blank. She and Amira slipped out the door quietly leaving the two of them alone.

An eternity passed before Georgie spoke. 'I'm so sorry, Jed.' She blinked back more tears.

Jed pulled her into his arms and hugged her hard. 'You have nothing to apologise for. These things happen.'

But even as he comforted her, questions ping-ponged through her head. Why? How? What had she done wrong? Should she have been resting instead of working fulltime? And should she have stopped running?

A few minutes later Amira stepped back in the room. 'We

should chat about your options.'

Georgie stared at her, not understanding. 'Options?' she asked, voice cracking. 'What options?'

There was only supposed to be one option. Having a baby.

***

Once everyone in town found out they'd lost their baby—word spread within hours of it happening—the townsfolk of Glengarrick did what they did best: they rallied around him and Georgie. Family, friends, acquaintances, and people Jed didn't even know, reached out to them, sharing their own stories of grief and loss and hope, and of rainbow babies. It only partially helped ease the pain of their loss. Even though the baby hadn't been planned, he had been very much wanted.

One Saturday morning, about two months after the miscarriage, just before Christmas, Jed suggested they head to the beach for the day. It had been hard getting her out of the house and he knew he needed to shake things up a bit. Hopefully what he had planned would work. She'd always loved the beach.

'This spot okay with you?' he asked, after turning off the main road and pulling into the car park overlooking the water. The sun shone high in a perfect blue sky.

'Looks good to me,' Georgie replied with a small smile.

He could hear in her voice that she was trying hard to be

enthusiastic for his sake.

'If it's too windy, we can walk around a bit further. It's more sheltered over there.'

Grabbing a picnic blanket from the boot, he handed it to her, before pulling out an insulated picnic bag. He took her hand and they walked across the grass towards the beach. When they got to a place where the grass met the sand, they put the blanket and basket in the dunes.

Georgie slipped off her shoes then turned and gave him a look he hadn't seen in two months since they lost little Robbie. They'd named him after her dad.

'Wanna race?' she asked.

Before he had time to respond, she took off, kicking up sand behind her as she ran.

'Slowpoke,' she called back over her shoulder.

For a second, he stood, rooted to the ground in astonishment, before chasing after her towards the water. He arrived at her side, panting, moments later. 'What was the rush?'

'I wanted to see if you'd lost your fitness since you stopped playing footy.' She dashed off again into the shallows.

He followed and kicked icy water at her.

She squealed. 'That's not fair.' She bent and scooped water in her hands and threw it back at him.

Soon they were both drenched and laughing like toddlers. Relief washed over him. It was so good to hear her laugh. From the look in her eyes, she knew it too.

Without a word, he took her hand and they started walking, traipsing the length of the beach and back, pausing occasionally to admire a dog, or chat to someone about the weather. Mostly they strolled in comfortable silence, letting the fresh salty air fill their souls again.

'This has been nice,' she said an hour later. 'Exactly what we needed. I haven't been to the beach in ages.' She bent to pick up a shell and turned it in her hands, admiring it. 'This is so pretty.' She wiped the sand off it before slipping it into the pocket of her shorts.

He nudged her with his hip. 'You going to start a shell collection?'

'No. I'm collecting memories.' She smiled. 'I'm going to collect mementos to remind me of good days. Today is a good day and I don't want to forget it. This,' she indicated the beach, 'is perfect. And so is spending time with you. I'm sorry I've been so difficult to live with lately.'

'Oh, sweetheart. You haven't. It's been a difficult season for both of us.'

'But at least we're together,' she said, taking his hand again.

He squeezed it. 'Always.'

They arrived back at the spot they'd left the picnic basket and blanket. 'Are you happy to sit here?'

When she nodded, Jed took the blanket and spread it on the sand, near the dunes, out of the wind. They sank down into the loose sand and lay side by side, barely touching as they stared up into the azure blue sky.

As a cloud drifted overhead, Georgie sighed. 'I don't remember the last time I felt this relaxed,' she said, her voice breaking slightly. 'Even before I was pregnant.'

'It's been a long time for me too,' he agreed. So much had happened in such a short space of time. Since retiring from football his entire life had changed.

'Do you think we'll ever get over losing Robbie?' she asked.

He shifted position and rested on an elbow so he could look her in the eyes. 'Honestly? No, I don't think we will. But I don't think we're supposed to. He's part of our story. Part of us.'

'We have lots to our story, don't we?'

He stroked her hair. 'Yeah. We do.'

She looked up at him. 'Do you ever think back to that night of the storm when you found me in the creek?'

'Often.' He chuckled. 'Up to that point, it was the best night of my life.'

She rolled her eyes. 'I'm not talking about *that*. If you hadn't come along when you did, I could have died.'

They lay in silence, on their backs, watching the clouds cross the sky as they silently relived the memories of that night.

'I was so scared when you got knocked out,' she said. 'Then when you got hit again playing football, it was awful, like it was happening again.'

Jed held his breath. He'd carried a secret for too long and it was time to tell her.

He took her hand in his. 'When I got knocked out at the start of this year, I had a lot of CT scans and MRIs of my brain. The doctors told me they could see from my scans that I'd been concussed before. They were worried about something called SIS—Second Impact Syndrome. I'd never heard of it. It's when someone sustains a second head injury before the symptoms of the first head injury have fully resolved. They asked me if I'd ever been knocked out and I told them I hadn't. The club doctor pulled me aside later and questioned me too. He asked if I'd ever had concussion when I was younger. I lied. I didn't tell him about that night.'

She sat up and turned to face him. 'Why didn't you say something?'

'We promised we'd never tell anyone what happened that night.'

'But you're saying if you got another knock to the head you could have been seriously injured or…' Her voice trailed off.

'That's why I knew I had to retire. After the second knock, I couldn't risk it because I knew it was actually the third bad concussion I'd had where I'd lost consciousness.'

Georgie sucked in a long breath.

He watched her join the dots and knew what was going through her head. He sat up and took her hands in his. 'It wasn't your fault. It was an accident. I chose to play AFL and it's a tough, physical game. It was a risk I took knowing about the concussion from the tree branch.'

'But if I hadn't agreed to lie and cover for Zara, I wouldn't have been driving that night and you wouldn't have had to rescue me. And the tree wouldn't have knocked you out.'

'This is not your fault, Georgie. If anyone is to blame, it's me. I shouldn't have lied to the coaches and doctors.'

Tears filled her eyes. 'I am so sorry. I feel like somehow it's my fault.'

He gently took her chin and tilted her head back to look at him. 'It wasn't. It happened. An accident. We had no way of knowing it would contribute to the end of my career ten years later. But regardless, I'm grateful I was there that night to rescue you. If I hadn't been…' He shuddered. 'Well, we wouldn't be here now.'

Tears trickled down her cheeks. 'You were my hero and I could never thank you. I could never tell anyone how incredible you were that night. Not even Zara.'

He gently wiped away her tears. 'You didn't need to. Anyway, I didn't do it to become a hero.'

She sniffed. 'I will never ever forget what you did. You saved my life that night, Jed.'

He grinned. 'And I'll never forget how you thanked me.'

She laughed and the tension in the air eased. 'Is that all you think about?'

'Pretty much.' He leant back on his arms. 'Isn't sex with me all *you* think about?'

'Um. No.'

'What *do* you think about?'

She became instantly serious. 'I think about the future. What it looks like.' She bit her lip. 'Whether we'll try for another baby.'

'Is that what you want?'

She nodded.

He kissed her forehead. 'Then, when you're ready, we can try again.'

He pulled away, reached into the picnic basket, and pulled out a small box he'd hidden earlier that day. He'd been unsure of the timing of this moment, but he'd put the box there, just in case things had gone as well as he'd hoped.

They'd been better.

He stood and looked down at her.

'I was going to do this properly later tonight when the sun sets, but I need to do it now.'

As he knelt before her and opened the box, revealing the ring he'd bought for her, Georgie's mouth fell open.

'Will you marry me, Georgina Purcell?'

Tears pooled in her eyes. She nodded vigorously, unable to speak.

He stood and pulled her up, then took the ring from the box and slipped it onto her finger. It was a perfect fit. Cupping her face in his hands, he pressed his lips against hers. 'I love you so much, Georgie. Now and forever.'

'I love you too.'

Chapter 24

The next few months flew by and it wasn't long before their wedding day arrived. As they were already living together, they'd decided there was no point in a long engagement.

The August sun was high in the sky and the breeze was cool without being icy, yet not quite strong enough to shake the remaining leaves from the ornamental pear trees lining the long driveway to Jed's farm. After announcing their engagement, Michelle had insisted they move to the farm and she'd bought herself a unit in a retirement village in Stockton. Close enough to see them often, without being too close.

They'd picked this weekend for the wedding because all their friends would be home for the Grand Final. But this year, neither Jed nor Georgie would be going to the game. Instead, they'd be jetting off on their honeymoon in the Maldives.

Jed had jokingly asked if she'd wanted to run the Peak to Pub on the morning of their wedding day, and for a second she'd considered it, until Zara had freaked out and said no, she had the hairdresser coming at nine.

Georgie peered through the plantation shutters of their bedroom window. In the garden, wedding guests gathered. She smiled. Everyone they loved was here. In fact, judging by the number of cars lining the driveway, the entire town had come for a look.

Heart bursting with excitement, Georgie couldn't wait for the moment she saw the love in Jed's eyes as she joined him under the arbour and became his wife.

In the sunlight, the new trees she and Jed had planted looked like silent sentinels. The driveway, once pot-holed and narrow, had been widened and new gravel laid. Not just in preparation for their wedding, but for the first group of students who would arrive in February next year.

Jed's efforts over the past few months to transform the property were astounding. What had been a sad and neglected farmhouse was now a modern homestead. Off to the side were the black painted shipping containers that the builders were busily transforming into dormitory style accommodation for the students. They still had a lot more work to do on the gardens, but it was all coming together perfectly. Georgie was so happy for Jed as his vision for the farm took place.

Lifting the skirt of her floor length gown off the ground, she walked gingerly across the gravel driveway towards the flower covered arbour that had been erected at the end of a row of bare branched fruit trees in the orchard. She stopped a short distance from the entrance to the garden and waited patiently while Zara fussed with the back of her dress, spreading out the long train. The intricate beading on her ivory silk gown caught the dappled sunshine and shimmered like diamonds on water.

'So much for keeping things simple,' Zara said.

Georgie smoothed the front of the gown. 'It's not too much is it?'

'Definitely not.'

'You think Jed will like it?'

Zara grinned. 'No doubt about it. He'll love it.'

'And I look okay?'

'Trust me, you look unbelievable.'

Georgie inhaled and exhaled. 'I didn't expect to be so nervous.'

She and Jed had planned for only their immediate family to attend a modest wedding ceremony and dinner, but Zara had joined forces with Michelle and Jane and over a hundred people were gathered, including invited members of the media. What was supposed to be a simple wedding had morphed into something elaborate, yet oddly, Georgie didn't mind. She hoped Jed wasn't too upset about it. He'd told her he didn't want a celebrity-style wedding and yet with some media there, there was every chance their photos would appear in the paper or on the news.

'I'm sure it's normal to be anxious,' Zara assured her. 'It's your wedding day.'

'What if I trip while I'm walking towards him? Or I forget my vows?'

'Would you stop worrying, Georgie Porgie? You'll be fine.'

On hearing her nickname, Georgie relaxed. Trust Zara to bring her back to earth. Clutching her bridal bouquet in both hands, she focused on her breathing.

'You ready?' Mum asked, appearing at her side. She reached for Georgie's hand and tucked it in the crook of her arm.

Georgie nodded through a blur of happy tears. 'Ready as I'll ever be.'

'Dad would be so proud of you,' Jane said.

'Thanks, Mum.'

Moments later Georgie spied Jed, beaming at her from where he stood under the arbour. Her breath caught in the back of her throat. He looked handsome in his dark suit and white open necked shirt. She walked slowly towards him, unable to take her eyes off him as the music being played by the violin quartet swelled around her.

The next few minutes passed in a haze and soon it was time for their vows.

'Georgie Purcell, you are my lover, my best friend and now my wife. Thank you for saying yes. Today, in front of everyone we love, I give you everything I have and everything that I am. All my dreams, my hopes, my fears. I give you my triumphs and my failures. I trust you with my heart and know it is safe with you. I will do whatever I can to be worthy of your love.

'And if we face times of struggle or hardship or difficulty again, I promise you can depend on me to support you, to protect you and to love you unconditionally, no matter what. I adore you. It's that simple and that true. You are the epitome of everything I have searched for in another human being. There isn't a soul on this earth who has ever made me feel half the person I am when I'm with you. Because of you in my life I will forever be in love. You mean the world to me and I promise to love you, cherish you and honour you always.'

Jed slipped the slender diamond encrusted band onto her finger and raised it to his lips, sealing his promises with a kiss.

Georgie swallowed past the lump in her throat and willed herself not to cry and ruin her makeup. She'd never felt happier in her life.

'Jed Delaney, you are my lover, my best friend and now my husband. Thank you for saying yes. Today in front of everyone we love and hold dear, I give you my heart. My feet shall run because of you. My feet shall dance because of you. My heart shall beat because of you. My eyes will see because of you. My mind will dream because of you. And I shall love because of you. You are my inspiration. You are the magic of my days. You have helped me to laugh and you have taught me to love. You have offered me a safe place and given me wings to fly and breath to sing my own song. Each day I fall more in love with you. You are mine forever, lodged in my heart.'

She took Jed's left hand and they both held their breath as she wriggled his ring over the knuckle. When it was finally in position, they exhaled in a rush. The crowd chuckled.

'You may now kiss the bride,' the celebrant said.

'About time,' Jed murmured before lowering his head and kissing her tenderly.

Georgie closed her eyes and welcomed his kiss and the love it represented. As cheers and wolf whistles rang out from their friends and family, she tilted her head back as Jed deepened the kiss. She would never get tired of this.

After they signed all the paperwork, Jed took her hand and together they walked down the aisle and into the pale sunshine.

***

The wedding reception that night was picture perfect. A huge white marquee had been erected beside the old woolshed. One side was left open so guests could look out over the paddocks and enjoy the views of the setting sun. Fairy lights were strung between the bare branched fruit trees in the orchard creating a magical effect. Inside the marquee, portable gas heaters and a large potbelly fire kept guests toasty warm. The white-clothed tables surrounded a small dance floor and were finished with white place settings and silver-plated cutlery. Jazz singers crooned softly over the sound system. It was classy without looking like they'd hired a wedding planner, which in fact they had.

Jed remained glued to her side for the entire night, his smile never leaving his face. The only time they were separated was when they received a congratulatory hug or handshake from one of their friends.

The entire gang was there to celebrate with them. Everyone except Zara's partner, Kath. They had recently split after Kath announced she didn't want to have children. Charlie was their master of ceremonies and he'd spent the entire night chatting to Annabel, who was acting as Jed's unofficial Best Woman. Neither of them had wanted a bridal party.

After dinner had been served and eaten, Charlie announced Jed had a surprise for everyone.

A shiver ran down Georgie's spine. She sent Jed a look and mouthed, 'What?'

He downed his glass of champagne and winked at her.

'What are you doing?' she whispered, leaning in towards him. 'I thought we'd agreed to skip the whole "first dance" thing?'

He gave her another mischievous wink before moving to the centre of the dance floor and beckoning with one finger for her to join him. The guests formed a circle and clapped in anticipation.

'What are you doing?' Georgie asked as she walked towards him. She had to work hard to act annoyed because she actually couldn't stop laughing at the cheeky look on her husband's face.

'You promised you wouldn't embarrass me.'

'You promised me we wouldn't have a big wedding.'

They laughed.

Jed pulled a chair out from a table, shrugged off his jacket, and lay it over the back of the chair. Georgie scanned the room to see if anyone else knew what was happening, but everyone wore expectant looks.

The sound of an acoustic guitar came through the speakers and Georgie gulped when she recognised the opening strains of *Shallow*. Jed held out his hand, inviting her to come and sit on the chair. His eyes crinkled with laughter. 'Thought we could end the night with some karaoke.'

She shook her head.

'But you love it,' he said, grinning at her.

'I don't know the words.'

'Liar,' he teased. 'You told me you've watched the film dozens of times.' He pointed to a large screen that someone had erected. 'The words will come up there. Just sing along. You can do this. It's like the night at the pub.'

She swallowed and shook her head again.

'Breathe, Georgie. And trust me,' he whispered in her ear. 'I'll never let you fall.'

Her legs propelled themselves towards him and she took the microphone Charlie thrust into her hands. Perching on the edge of the chair she faced Jed while he started to sing the opening lyrics of the song.

Tears filled her eyes at how beautifully he sang and when it was her turn, she didn't hold back, but gave it everything she had, not taking her eyes off him as she ignored the oohs and aahs and the flashes from cameras popping around them.

When the song ended, she could barely hear herself think over the sound of the cheers from the crowd. Jed took the microphone from her shaking hands and set it on the floor before taking her in his arms, forming the traditional waltz pose.

Georgie stiffened. 'I can't dance while everyone's watching.'

'You just sang your heart out while everyone was watching. All you need to do is relax and let me lead you.'

She dragged in a deep lungful of air and nodded. 'Okay.'

He gave her a crooked smile as he pulled her securely against him. It made her laugh. He was clearly loving every minute of being the centre of attention.

'Do you remember my vows?' he asked as he slowly propelled her across the dance floor. 'I promised all you need to do is put one foot in front of the other and follow me.'

She nodded.

'So that's what this is all about. Trust me and let me lead you and I promise I'll never take you anywhere that's too far out of your comfort zone.'

She looked up into his eyes and when he leaned down and planted a soft kiss on her mouth, her chest tightened.

'I love you so much.'

'And I love you too.'

His eyes bore into hers and she saw the truth in his words. He kissed her again and she snuggled closer, burying her face in his neck.

'Is it time to leave yet?' he whispered.

She giggled. 'It's not even nine o'clock. And we haven't cut the cake or had the speeches.'

He groaned. 'Surely no-one will notice if we slip out.'

She pointed to the photographer who was still snapping photos of them. 'I reckon they'll notice if we've gone.'

Sharing a smile, they continued to dance the night away, oblivious to everyone around them.

Epilogue

August, the following year

'Hurry up, Mum, or we'll be late,' Georgie called out.

'Coming,' Jane called back.

Georgie grabbed Mum's coat and put the esky and thermos in the car. Five minutes later they were on their way into town to the footy ground for the Grand Final. As the new coach of the Glengarrick *Saints*, Jed had gone ahead hours earlier. Halfway through the season, Frank, the previous coach, had suffered a heart attack. Despite a full recovery, he'd made the decision to hang up his boots. Jed had been the logical choice to coach the side.

Georgie and her mother parked as close as they could get to the ground, hopped out and walked down the road, chatting with other locals about the upcoming game. It seemed an even bigger crowd had turned out than two years ago and Georgie spotted a channel seven news car and a man with a camera on his shoulder. She would have thought by now Jed would be old news, but the media still loved him, especially after he'd coached this team to a win every week. There was no way they wouldn't win today.

She smiled to herself. After today, hopefully they'd have

another great "good news" story.

After paying the entrance fee at the gate, they headed towards the club rooms. Georgie didn't expect to see Jed and was surprised to hear him call her name.

She turned and he slid his arms around her waist before planting a long kiss on her lips. 'Happy anniversary my lover. Sorry we have to spend it here.'

'I don't mind at all.' She kissed him again.

When they broke apart, Jed greeted his mother-in-law with a hug and a kiss on the cheek. 'Hi, Jane.'

'When are you going to call me Mum?' Jane asked.

Georgie chuckled at the blush on her mother's cheeks. Jane worshipped the ground Jed walked on.

Jed winked at Georgie before looping his arm through her mums. 'I thought you might prefer it if I called you Nana. Or would you prefer Nanny? Or Grandma?'

Jane stopped and looked at him, mouth and eyes wide.

Georgie grinned at the look on her mother's face.

'Are you? Are we? Is he?' she stammered, turning from Georgie back to Jed.

Jed pulled Georgie in close and draped an arm over her shoulder. 'Hope you don't have any plans this Christmas, Mum, because we're going to need someone to babysit.'

If you enjoyed this book, please click here for the next book in the series: Settle the Score

Also by Nicki Edwards

Escape to the Country Series (Medical Romance)

Book #1: Intensive Care

Book #2: Emergency Response

Novella: Operation White Christmas

Book #3: Life Support

Book #4: Critical Condition

Novella: Operation Mistletoe Magic

The Peppercorn Project

One More Song

Holding Onto Hope

Second Chance Christmas

Coming Soon

Novella: Lake of Dreams

Off the Field Series

Book #2: Settle The Score

Book #3: The Last Quarter

About the Author

Nicki is a city girl with a country heart. Growing up on acreage outside Geelong in Victoria, Australia, Nicki spent her formative years riding horses, hand rearing lambs and pretending the neighbour's farm was her own. After spending three years in a regional town in New South Wales in her twenties, Nicki's love of country towns and rural life was further developed.

Nicki's dream is to one day escape to the country and live on land surrounded by horses, dogs, cows and sheep. Unfortunately, until (or if) that happens, Nicki will continue to live vicariously through the lives of the characters in the books she loves to read and write.

A voracious reader, Nicki always wanted to be an author. After returning to university as a mature aged student to study nursing, Nicki juggled full time study, part time work and raising four small children to achieve her dream of becoming a nurse. But her other dream—the dream to write—never left, and in January 2015 Nicki had her first book published.

Nicki now divides her time between writing, working as a nurse in General Practice or riding her new horse, Monty.

Nicki and her husband Tim have four young adult children, two spoiled border collies (#mollyandindie) and an ancient Burmese cat called Roxy.

To stay up to date with her latest releases, please visit Nicki's website: http://www.nickiedwardsauthor.com or find her on Facebook or Instagram where she spends far too much time!